Erotica Sex Stories for Men

Taboo Daddy Explicit Erotica Sex Stories for Lesbians, Reverse Harem Short Romance with Forbidden Younger Women Collection

Sasha Coleman

COPYRIGHT

This document is geared towards providing exact and reliable information with regard to the topic and issue covered. The publication is sold with the idea that the publisher is not required to render accounting, officially permitted or otherwise qualified services. If advice is necessary, legal or professional, a practiced individual in the profession should be ordered. - From a Declaration of Principles which was accepted and approved equally by a Committee of the American Bar Association and a Committee of Publishers and Associations.

Contents

THE TUTOR

Claudia:

As so often in the past few weeks, I was sitting on the bed with my best friend Lisa in my room, which was not fully furnished. Having met her was the best thing that had happened to me in a long time in my life. When I moved with my parents two months ago and came to my new school, I didn't know anyone at first. But I got on well with Lisa straight away, she showed me the school and the city, through her I also got in touch with her clique and through her I got over Tim, from whom I separated shortly before my move would have. Last but not least, she also got me a tutor in my math problem - her father, who, as it happened, taught math at a vocational school. So we sat together again

Thomas:

Out of breath I lay next to my wife Carolin in bed, my arm around her. she stroked, just as exhausted and with a dreamy look through my hair. "Wow honey, what was wrong with you today?" she asked smiling, "I haven't seen you so passionately in a long time." I gave her a tender kiss on the mouth and looked her in the eye. "Well, it's the last time for the next two weeks when you're going on vacation with your friends tomorrow." I answered her. But it was really a shame - only recently we got on really well after a somewhat difficult time, both in everyday life and in bed. She seemed to have guessed my thoughts because she lovingly turned to me nestled against me and gave me a passionate kiss. "I'm sorry too, honey. But the vacation has been booked for a long time, and it's only been two weeks." I returned her kiss and our tongues started performing a hot dance as we stroked and hugged each other. "It's only good," I said in a short kiss break, "but I'm going to treat you to a vacation, and I hope it will be nice for you." Thank you, there was another hot kiss from Caro, and gradually we slept arm in arm a.

Claudia:

The next day around noon I packed up my maths things. I had already spent half a morning solving exercise sheets and rereading notes from class, but it didn't help. In fact, I understood as little as I did all the time before, and wondered what Lisa's father could do great differently than my teachers. But it couldn't go on like this, so I quickly got dressed and brushed my teeth again. Since it was a hot day and I didn't feel like sweating while I was studying, I put an airy summer dress over my underwear, took my backpack and drove to the Mullers. When I arrived, I rang the bell and tried to put on a friendly smile. Lisa's father didn't really have to notice that I had no desire where he was so nice to help me. It took some time before it opened, so at first I thought he wasn't home, but when he was standing in front of me, I just had a thought - "WOW!"

Thomas:

So she turned the corner. I waved after her one last time, then she couldn't see me anymore. Her friends had come 5 minutes ago to pick up Caro. A little depressed I lie back in the house, sit down in the living room and switch on the television. I paid no attention to the program. I wondered why I was so sad, after all, it wasn't the first time that Caro went on vacation alone. But I just wanted to have her with me right now, spend every second with her. Only after a few moments did I register that the doorbell had rung. I didn't really want to see anyone, but I decided to open it. A blond girl, about my daughter's age, was waiting at the door, I guessed. "Oh hello!" I greeted her, "

Claudia:

I wasn't prepared for such a sight. Why hadn't Lisa said that her father was such an attractive man? With his short brown hair, soft skin, and above all his incredible dark eyes, he just looked incredibly sexy! Only at that moment he seemed a little confused. Only after a few moments did he seem to remember that we had an appointment, made a quick apology and asked me into the house. I already knew the apartment from my visits to Lisa and just went after him into the living room. What I could see in spite of jeans indicated a very crisp bottom. He quickly got something to drink for us, and I sat down at the table and spread out my math things.

Thomas:

Fortunately, Claudia didn't seem to resent my forgetfulness. In all my tribulations about Caro's departure, I had completely forgotten the tutoring. Wildly determined to make up for it, I quickly got a Coke from the kitchen and vowed to give everything to help her. When I came back, I noticed her with my senses for the first time, and had to realize that Lisa had a very pretty friend, with a very sweet smile and bright, deep blue eyes, and a body that was not to be scoffed at. I quickly got my thoughts back and sat down with her. First I asked them what they were doing at school, where they saw their problems, and let me show them their documents. We worked very intensively and after a short time I wondered

Claudia:

After Thomas, who asked me to call him that, had apologized a few more times and I made it clear to him that it was not a problem, he finally caught up and we turned to my maths stuff. It was just amazing. His explanations and examples just sounded so much more plausible than anything in school. Or was it just that I felt so comfortable in his presence? Math was suddenly the easiest in the world ... Well, that was probably a little exaggerated, but after a short time I had the feeling that I understood most of what he explained. I kept glancing at him a little, and it became clearer every minute - I wanted this man!

Thomas:

The longer our tutoring session lasted, the more fun it was for me. I had been tutoring students a couple of times, but I had never felt so good with anyone. And the whole thing also distracted me from Carolin. In addition, Claudia was really a nice girl, and as I said, a very attractive girl. When I looked over at her at one point while she was sitting over a task, I noticed for the first time what wonderful breasts she had. I caught myself looking a second or third time. In addition, they were really wonderfully emphasized by their dress. They were larger than my wife's, but seemed wonderfully firm and tight. I couldn't stop my pants from moving a bit and forced myself

Claudia:

I had to make every effort not to think about Thomas all the time, which was not easy, since he was sitting right next to me. What was wrong with me I loved my best friend's father. I knew he was still married, and according to Lisa, her parents were happy again. What should it do, he wouldn't notice me anyway ... Or? Did I make a mistake or did he stole glances at my stem. I decided to help out a little and leaned forward very far so that he would have a wonderful look in my neckline and watched him inconspicuously again and again.

Thomas:

Our hour was coming to an end, and I was catching my eyes wandering over to her wonderful neckline more and more. Did she notice anything? I quickly looked back somewhere else, but could not prevent the sight of it from exciting me. So I was somewhat happy when the tutoring was over. I told her how happy I was with her and that I was sure that she no longer needed to be afraid of math. She thanked me with a little kiss on my cheek. I felt her soft lips, sucked in her fragrance. Again there was this attraction that she had on me. "Control yourself Thomas!" I called out to myself and accompanied her to the door. When I ran after her, I found that her butt also seemed to be perfect.

Claudia:

I was a little disappointed when Thomas told me that the hour for today was over. But I hadn't left him cold, I sensed that. He had tried not to show anything, but his eyes could not be missed. And when I kissed him, just on the cheek, of course, he twitched slightly. I smiled at him and ran to the door in front of him. I was sure that his eyes were on my bottom. We made an appointment for the next hour two days later, and with anticipation I got on my bike and went home. The whole evening my thoughts were around Thomas. When I lay in my bed, I couldn't stand it any longer.

Thomas:

When Claudia was gone, I had to sit down for a moment. I didn't expect anything like that. How could this girl get me out of the box? I decided to take another bike ride to change my mind, and in fact, when I got home exhausted, my hormones were back to normal. But Claudia had done something to me, because when I lay in bed at night and wanted to sleep, I could only think of her, and the more I resisted it, the worse it got. The image of her flawless body in my head kept my cock growing. As if by itself, my hand slipped into my shorts and lay against my stiff member.

Claudia:

I couldn't help it. I didn't want anything else. I shoved my hand into my pink panties and stroked my pussy dreamily. I felt how the thought of Thomas had already made her wet and excited. I touched my sensitive clit and moaned softly into the covers. No man had triggered such feelings in me for a long time. Not even Tim had been able to do that in the past few months of our relationship. I penetrated deeply with two fingers and immediately began to finger myself quickly and lustfully. My whole body was flooded with waves of pleasure, I reached to the side in my bedside table and took out my red dildo.

Thomas:

I felt that my cock was already really hard and that a few drops of pleasure had already made their way out. I started to jerk my cock full of lust. I always had Claudia's face, her breasts, her bottom in front of my eyes. It had been ages since I had satisfied myself with another woman. Even when Carolin and I didn't get on well, there was never another woman for me, and now that ... Slowly I moved my hand up and down on my piston, with the other I stroked my bulging one Eggs.

Claudia:

Without hesitation I pushed my red friend deep into my wet hole. If only it were Thomas' cock that entered me! Again and again I pushed him deep inside, massaging my chest with my other hand, how hard my nipples were! As if out of my senses I moaned my lust, Thomas name came over my lips again and again, I twisted on my bed, the dildo filled me so much ... I felt how my body always orgasm came closer, how my pussy started to twitch wildly, I cried out, hot waves flashed through me, I came, I came as I haven't in a long time ...

Thomas:

I worked my throbbing cock faster and faster. Constantly the pictures of Claudia in my head, I could almost smell them, it made me feel hotter and hotter. My cock slipped through my hand, more and more of my pleasure juice was already dripping out of it. I was on fire, I could have screamed with pleasure. I felt the juice rise from my eggs, my cock rose, and with a loud groan I squirted out my juice, the first load came in a high arc on my stomach, it came more and more, I had not been so violent for a long time sprayed more.

Claudia:

I couldn't wait to see Thomas again. The next day passed so slowly, my thoughts knew only one again - HIM. As so often, I met Lisa again this afternoon. I already had a guilty conscience about her. I owed her my new life to her, she was my best friend and had no idea of ??my thoughts. Of course, she also asked me what the tutoring with her father was like, I just told her that I had made great progress with him. Still, we had a great day together, went shopping a bit into the city. If she had known that the sexy mini skirt I bought was for her father. I could hardly sleep at night, just had to think about the next day ...

Thomas:

The next morning I woke up feeling more than bad. What was wrong with me My wife was just a day away, and I was drawn to such thoughts by such a young thing. I was in a mid-life crisis, as Caro had accused me of in our worse times. Self-doubt gnawed at me all day, so I could hardly concentrate on my work. How should I survive the next day? Should I call Claudia, give her some excuse why I had to cancel the local aid. On the other hand, I could really help her in school. And what would Lisa think if I stopped teaching after an hour? The next morning I made my decision - I would give Claudia tuition, I would pull myself together and resist her charms! With that in mind, I went to the door when the doorbell rang.

Claudia:

I woke up excited the next morning. The school seemed to take longer than it did on normal days. But today shouldn't be a normal day. When I got back home at noon, I hurriedly ate a few bites. I just couldn't get any more down. I took a long shower, because I wanted to smell good for Thomas. With difficulty I resisted the urge to do it myself in the shower. My pussy had to wait a little longer. I put on my new mini skirt. After much thought, I decided to wear a black thong underneath. Without it, I would have felt a little cheap. It was a hint of nothing. He just had to please Thomas. I also wore a white halter top and a matching bra. At last it was time, I got on my bike and drove to my crush. When he opened the door for me, he smiled sweetly at me and let me in. Oh, I love that smile! I ran into the living room in front of him and made sure that my butt also came into its own.

Thomas:

I opened the door and let Claudia in. I tried not to show anything to her and asked her into the living room. She ran wildly ahead of me. Damn, she looked good again, and that smell ... I forced myself to think about something else and so we started tutoring. To my surprise, she made no further attempts to provoke me and we made very good progress. I was pleased to see that, like me, she was apparently only interested in improving her math performance. As if in flight, the hour was over again, she packed up her things and got up. She smiled at me and thanked me for my great help. And then, without warning, she took a step towards me and before I could fight back she was sitting on my lap with her lips pressed against mine. Completely shocked, I let it happen for a moment. WOW, what lips, so soft and full! Her tongue ventured into my mouth. I felt her wonderfully feminine body very close to me and I couldn't help it, stormily I returned her kiss.

Claudia:

I decided to take it slow at first. I felt his insecurity, his tornness. So I initially concentrated on tutoring, and like last time we made good progress. His explanations were just great. I could feel him loosening up over time and decided to weigh him in safety first. When we finished the lesson, I went all out. I sat on his lap and started kissing him. Our lips met, I wrapped my arms around his neck and to my surprise and delight he returned the kiss. It was a dream kiss, his tongue greedily made contact with mine and I could feel his hands on my bottom. I gently stroked his neck hair and pressed my breasts against him.

Thomas:

I sucked Claudia into myself with all my senses. Our mouths performed a hot dance, I clawed my hands in their firm buttocks and kneaded it with passion. Slowly I pushed her skirt a little higher and felt her bottom with my fingers. She moaned softly in my mouth and nestled her youthful body against me. It was a long time since I had felt such a desire for a woman, not even with Caro ... Caro! ran through my thoughts. What was i doing here That couldn't happen. Gentle, but still determined. I pushed her off my lap and looked at her seriously. Her look told me that she hadn't expected it. "I think it's better if you go now," I told her, handing her backpack.

Claudia:

I enjoyed our kisses full of lust. I could feel how much Thomas wanted me. His hands pampered my half-naked buttocks, and our tongues kept playing hot games. I slowly moved my hand down from his head, over his back, but suddenly he broke our kiss and pushed me away. I looked at him in surprise, but he seemed very serious. What was suddenly going on with him, I had done something wrong. In a serious voice he asked me to go. I didn't know how to react, but he was so determined, so clear that I decided to follow his request. I could have cried on the way home, so disappointed I was. But I vowed never to give up. The very next day, when Lisa was training,

Thomas:

I was relieved to see that she made no attempt to seduce me any further. I no longer accompanied her to the door, but made myself a glass of whiskey and dropped onto the sofa. But what just happened ?? Within a minute I had overturned all my resolutions and had to think of Claudia again. The kiss had just been so wonderful, just thinking about it made me horny again. I sipped the glass in one sip and kept thinking about Claudia. My pants are stretched to the brim, and everything is spinning in my head. Finally I couldn't stand it anymore and got into my car and drove to Claudia. I hoped her parents wouldn't be there, but even if I did, I would come up with some excuse.

Claudia:

I was about to go to bed. The experience with Thomas had totally killed me. I couldn't understand that he had let me down. So I didn't even want to go to the door when I heard the doorbell ringing, but finally I got up to look. I opened the door in a bad mood and when I saw Thomas standing there I was speechless. I think I stared at him pretty stupid, but he didn't pay any attention to it, but asked me if I was alone. I nodded and suddenly he came up to me, pushed me into the apartment and started kissing me. His hands were everywhere, exploring my body through clothing. He kicked the front door with one foot and pushed me against the opposite wall. I was still paralyzed and just let him do it. His kisses were so full of passion, slowly I started to join in. We licked wildly, I put my arms around his neck and caressed him tenderly.

Thomas:

I was crazy about this girl! I wanted to soak it up with skin and hair. I had not felt such passion in me for a long time. I didn't know which part of her perfect body I should stroke first. From her shoulders, my hands moved gently down her sides, over her hips. She stood with her back to the wall and nestled close to me. I felt her firm breasts press against me. Our tongues wrapped around each other, our lips united, we smacked gently smacking away. I slipped my hands a bit under her top and stroked her soft skin. I could feel her goosebumps and moan softly in my mouth.

Claudia:

His hands were so incredibly tender and gentle to me. He knew exactly where to stroke me. I also slowly let my hands go on a journey. I slipped it under his shirt and stroked his back. I slowly pushed my hands up and down, circling them on his back, caressing his spine with his fingertips. We melted closer and closer together, and finally I put my hands on his buttocks and hugged him tightly to me. Even through our clothes, I could feel his excitement and carefully rubbed against her. I felt him push towards me. I clenched my hands vigorously in his buttocks and started massaging them. His fingers crawled higher and higher on me, pushing up my top.

Thomas:

She had her sweet hands firmly clenched in my buttocks and I started to push her top up. My hands gently stroked her wonderfully soft skin until I reached the fabric of her bra. Carefully, with pleasure, I ran my fingers over it, moving ever closer to her bulging cups. I could feel her heartbeat, she was as excited as I was. Her breasts rose and fell in time with her breath, and then came the moment when I put my hands on her hills for the first time. What a feeling, I couldn't help but grab it hard and knead it gently.

Claudia:

I held my breath as he touched my breasts with his strong hands. Many men admired my breasts, but no one had ever touched them like Thomas! He kept squeezing her, massaging her vigorously. I could feel my sensitive nipples pressing against the fabric of the bras and reacting to every touch with a twitch like an electric flash. I could no longer suppress a moan and kissed him greedily on his lips again. I licked his lips with relish, continued to work with my lips, kissed him lovingly on the chin, and further over his neck. I traced his skin with his tongue and became more and more passionate.

Thomas:

We made each other more and more wild. She started to caress my neck while I still couldn't let go of her breasts. With a trembling hand, I undid the clasp of her bra, which fortunately was sitting in the front, and at the same time took off her bra and top. That girl was beautiful! Without hesitation I started stroking her bare breasts, trying to touch every millimeter. I played on her pink nipples, which stretched teasingly towards me. I could feel my skin flinching again and again. She sucked on my neck, kissed my shoulders, my upper arms. Her hot breath ensured that all my hairs stood up and I got goose bumps. With a jerk she also took off my top and passionately stroked my back.

Claudia:

The sight of my bare breasts only made my lover horny. We moaned at each other, enjoyed the contact with the partner. We were very close, I could feel every detail of his body. Especially how his hard cock rubbed against me through our clothes. I danced a little alongside him, made him feel my breasts and kissed his skin. The tip of my tongue snaked over his arm, up and down, over his shoulder, on his chest. He got goose bumps, I licked the little pimples on his skin. He put his hands on my head, stroked my hair and directed me to his chest. I gently licked his nipple, circled it with my tongue, and gripped my shoulders with my hands.

Thomas:

I enjoyed her treatment to the fullest. Claudia sucked on my nipples, alternately spoiled my two warts. Her fingernails in my shoulders caused a bittersweet pain that almost drove me crazy. I put my head back and gave myself fully to her. She really knew what she was doing, gently playing with her teeth on my hard nipples. I lovingly stroked her hair and scratched her neck. Despite the incredible pleasure we felt for each other, we took it slow. I let my hands slide down her back, stroking her in circular movements. In between, I kept touching the side of her breasts, her hips, until I reached her firm bottom and buried my hands in it. Every time

Claudia:

We became more and more united. His hands were so tender to me, I wanted to feel them everywhere. When he put her on my buttocks, I tensed my muscles and pressed my buttocks against him. He kneaded it fervently and moaned at me how beautiful I was. We dropped to the floor in quiet agreement, he lay on his back and I crouched between his legs and continued to pamper his chest. I put my hands on his thighs and gently stroked them up and down, always getting a little closer to his crotch. I could feel him getting more and more excited, he squirmed on the carpet below me. As I slowly kissed down from his chest, my lips exploring his stomach, I put my hand on his bump and massaged it gently. He groaned loudly and buried his hands in my hair. He was really tough.

Thomas:

We lay caressing ourselves intensely on the floor. Her tender little hand was on my crotch and my cock twitched with every touch. Claudia kissed my belly, licked my belly button with her tongue. I played with my hands in her long blonde hair. For a moment I thought about how much Carolin had always enjoyed pampering me with her lips. Claudia seemed to have noticed my short absence. "What is?" she asked me affectionately, and brought me back to the present with gentle strokes. To show her that I was completely with her, I pulled her up to me and gave her a hot French kiss. We licked each other wildly and I pushed my hands under her skirt on her bottom.

Claudia:

I felt that Thomas was somewhere else with his thoughts, probably with his wife. So I spoiled his best piece a little more intensely to bring him back to me. He skillfully covered up this brief uncomfortable moment by pulling me towards him and kissing me. I pressed my body against his and rubbed against him. His hands went under my skirt and lay on my bottom. It was such an intense feeling as he clasped his fingers in my buttocks and kneaded them vigorously. Shivering, I opened the button on his pants and shoved my hand inside. I finally took his hard cock in my hand and tenderly began to stroke it. I put my fingers around him and moved them back and forth. He groaned excitedly in my mouth and grabbed my butt a little tighter.

Thomas:

I jumped as if struck by lightning as she picked up my best piece and jerked it lovingly. Our kisses grew wild. I pushed her skirt a little higher and grabbed the ribbon of her sting and pulled a little. I carefully ran a finger through her column a few times, always moving a little further towards her column. I felt the heat she emitted and then rubbed my thumb once through her labia.

Claudia reared up and intensified the grip on my cock. Again and again she spoiled my sensitive, bulging eggs. I felt her tender fingers as they spoiled my step very gently and now rubbed my thumb over her clit.

Claudia:

When he pulled my panties at the back, the fabric snuggled tightly against my column. I was already soaking wet and felt the juice spread in the fabric. His fingers gently searched their way to my pussy. He teased my clitoris, which was now completely swollen, with his thumb and kept pushing another finger through my labia. I pressed my hand and enjoyed it to the fullest. Meanwhile his hard cock was pounding in my hand and I could see how much he liked it. He lifted his body up a bit and I took the opportunity to push pants and boxer shorts down for him. I looked at his fully grown cock for a moment and then picked it up again.

Thomas:

It was a tingling feeling to lie naked next to this hot girl. She spoiled my cock with both hands now, alternately she ran her fingers over it. I almost burst with excitement and pushed my index finger deeper into Claudia. Slowly I let him slide in and out again and again, which she thanked me with a lustful moan. It was a wonderful sound and only made me sharper on it. I added a second finger and introduced it to her. I carefully pressed her lips apart and irritated her pussy more and more. I could feel my cock trembling slightly and she transferred her lust to me. Her hand moved faster and faster on my cock, the first drops of lust spread on my glans.

Claudia:

I loved to feel his firm yet so soft and warm cock in my hand. I spoiled him more and more passionately, massaging his eggs with the other hand. His fingers circled deep in my pussy, he tried to feel and stroke every millimeter. We just kept pausing to kiss each other stormily. His other hand explored my body, slid over my back, onto my buttocks and caressed me there. As if by chance, his index finger strayed through my column for a brief moment. I sucked in the air and let it out with a hot groan. When he realized that I liked that, he kept running his finger through my Poritze while he massaged my pussy with the other hand.

Thomas:

For a long time I had wanted to spoil a woman's bottom more intensely. Her bottom had always been taboo for Carolin. So of course I enjoyed it all the more to let my finger penetrate Claudia's wonderful butt and see how she liked it. The more excited she became, the more she let my cock feel it. Her tender hand ecstatically caressed me. At some point she suddenly started sliding down on me. Her lips kissed against my skin, paused for a moment on my chest, and then continued to slide down. I trembled slightly, watching her impatiently. She licked my belly button with her tongue, I stroked her hair wildly and gently pressed her deeper.

Claudia:

Our game became more and more familiar. We instinctively knew what the other liked and wanted. I purposefully kissed his crotch, licked his stomach with relish, and rubbed his upper body with both hands. He looked at me with shiny eyes and I smiled at him. I seductively licked the tip of his tongue around his glans, whereupon he buried his hands in my hair and groaned loudly. I repeated the whole thing a few times, tasting his pleasure droplets and licking them with relish. He carefully pressed his member against me, I opened my lips a bit and let his acorn penetrate my mouth. I immediately sucked on him, slowly moving my head back and forth.

Thomas:

My hot lover skillfully began to spoil my cock with her mouth. She almost fooled me with her soft lips. I carefully pushed my cock towards her and at the same time pressed her head deeper. I continued to penetrate her mouth through her lips until I was in her as far as it would go. She held my cock like this for a moment, sucked on it and stroked my plump balls with both hands. I was so excited if I hadn't been careful I would have come in her mouth after a few seconds. So I concentrated on running my fingers through her hair and caressing her lovingly. Then Claudia started to move her head up and down. Again and again she released my cock up to the glans from her hot mouth. She constantly changed the pace. Sometimes my cock whizzed into her, bumping against her cheek from the inside, then she pushed it back very slowly and deeply. She tenderly played with her tongue. I groaned out of my mind. She kept looking at me from below. Her look almost drove me crazy.

Claudia:

Thomas was getting hotter with my caresses. I felt how he repeatedly pushed his cock against me from below. I smiled when I felt his passion. I put my thumb and index finger around his shaft and jerked him gently while his cock slid through my lips. I supported his efforts by moving my head up and down again and again so that his cock penetrated deeper into my mouth. I gently stroked his belly with my hand, carefully letting him feel my fingernails. The result was a hot purr from his mouth and another firm push into my mouth. I gasped softly and still enjoyed feeling it like this. His hands were buried in my hair, and his breath went faster and faster. Suddenly he took my head in my hands pulled his cock out of my mouth and looked at me. The glint in his eyes told me what he wanted, and I couldn't wait any longer either.

Thomas:

We both wanted it. Nothing could stop us, not my wife, not the age difference between us ... Like a cat, Claudia snaked up on me, I felt her with every fiber of my body, her breasts slid along me, her pussy came closer and closer to my cock . Our lips met again for a long and intense kiss, but then she reared up her torso, squatted on me and took my cock in my hand. A pleasant twitch ran through me, a few times she rubbed my acorn through her soaking wet labia. I could no longer hold back my moaning and pressed my pelvis against her from below. And then it finally happened! My acorn penetrated it, our bodies united. I could feel her tight young pussy tight around my cock

Claudia:

At last! My absolute dream man entered me! I slowly lowered my pelvis onto him, I enjoyed the moment, sucked him into me. He pushed against me from below, and Thomas pushed ever deeper into me. I let my pussy sink deeper and deeper until his cock was finally inside me. He put his hands on my buttocks and started kneading him like crazy, even giving me some light slaps. My lust increased and I started riding him rhythmically. At first I circled my pelvis only slowly, but we were both so horny that we soon set a wild pace. I kept pushing my pelvis up and down, and he rammed his cock towards me from below. My bottom slapped him hard every time.

Thomas:

I looked into Claudia's eyes from below. Saw the shine in them, their lust, their blazing desire! I let my eyes wander down her, over her dreamy breasts, which rocked up and down in sheer ecstasy. My hands reacted remotely, I placed them on her breasts and immediately started massaging them wildly. The feeling of holding those big firm breasts in my hand almost drove me crazy. I bit my lower lip, had to concentrate not to come. It hadn't happened to me for a long time. I squeezed her hemispheres firmly, over and over again. The girl on me thanked me by riding me harder and harder. My cock penetrated deeper into her, I was so deep inside her, it was so tight, so intense, I couldn't help but scream my lust out loud.

Claudia:

Thomas was so incredibly passionate! I had always loved being given special attention to my breasts. And yet his big, rough hands were the best I had ever felt in them. I leaned on his chest with both hands, even clawed my fingernails into it, I could see the spot blush slightly. He winced, but that only seemed to increase his arousal. He now took my two nipples, which were stretching hard and excited towards him, between his fingers and pulled them out. At first he was very careful, each time he pulled you tighter and let them whiz back. How did this man know exactly what I needed? My abdomen massaged his rock hard cock, our moans and screams were like music in my ears.

Thomas:

The bittersweet pain of her sharp fingernails in my skin made me shiver. My mind had long since said goodbye, I only reacted instinctively to the signals of her body, as she apparently did to me. My pleasure stick almost hurt from pent-up lust, and yet I keep driving it deep into her dripping wet hole. We treated ourselves to a little breather. Very slowly she rode on me, her breasts proudly stuck out, her head back. What a sight! I put an arm around her neck and pulled her down to me with a jerk, leaned towards her and pressed my lips to hers. We kissed, we ate each other completely, she played with her tongue deep in my mouth. Oh yes, Claudia could kiss!

Claudia:

Our bodies nestled tightly against each other. My breasts pressed against his chest, our lips were fused together, I pressed my pelvis very tightly against him, for a few minutes we just stayed that way and were one with the other. Our tongues chased each other, met, parted again. I wrapped my arms around him, buried my hands in his hair and stroked the back of his head. I could feel his hot breath in my mouth and slowly I started moving my pelvis again. His cock twitched, his whole body became more and more restless, he let himself fall back on the floor, put his hands on my hips and took the lead.

Thomas:

I enjoyed being close to Claudia. I had almost forgotten what it was like to get involved with a woman like that, and then also a young one. I moved her body along me, firmly gripped her hips and pressed it on me. I was so incredibly horny for her that it didn't take long and we had found our wild pace again. "Uuuhhjjaaa, Thomas !!" my little girl moaned at me and looked into my eyes. I grabbed her, rolled us around on the floor, and was now on top of her. She looked at me in surprise, but her gaze reflected pure lust. She wanted it, hard, deep! Her legs were spread wide, I lifted my pelvis, pulled myself almost completely out of her.

Claudia:

We rolled passionately on the floor. Thomas was now on top of me, and I wanted to be taken, my abdomen was on fire and cried out for redemption. I clung to his strong shoulders and the moment he rammed his pelvis hard against mine. I was more excited than ever in my life, my eyes went black and I saw stars. Several times he pressed his cock hard and mercilessly into my wet hole, then he eased a little and as if by itself we went into a passionate rhythm. His pleasure stick slid deep into me and I moved towards him from below. We kissed and loved each other, I could feel his hot breath and his deep, long moaning on my mouth. Thomas groaned my name and a wave of happiness flowed through me every time. It was mine, mine alone! My whole body pressed against him.

Thomas:

Oh god, this tightness! I enjoyed just pushing my cock hard into her wet gate. Her beautiful breasts nestled against my body, and together we moved more and more towards salvation. I took Claudia's sweet, soft face in my hands and looked deep into her shiny eyes. "You are so wonderful!" I whispered to her devotedly and in gratitude I was able to feel her full lips again. Her abdomen was getting tighter around my cock, she was moaning more and more uncontrollably. Several times she stretched her pelvis towards me from below, her hands buried in my skin, and I knew that she would soon be ready. I just wanted to make her happy, so I gave her some intense kisses and pushed my cock as deep as I could into my sweet lover.

Claudia:

I hardly knew where I was. With all my senses I concentrated on Thomas and let myself go. His tongue twitched in my mouth around mine, we moaned at each other. I could feel myself coming, I was savoring this moment, my body was pushing towards an incredible orgasm, everything about me was cramping, and then it happened, I exploded, I felt like I was taking off. I closed my eyes and enjoyed every moment, my juice poured out of me. Thomas kept going on and on, he didn't give me a moment of redemption. "Please, darling, don't stop, I love you!" it escaped from me and I pushed against it with all my strength.

Thomas:

My little one was in heaven and I wasn't going to let her come down so quickly. I lovingly pushed her on and on, and she pushed close to me. But suddenly, this sentence from her lips slightly open with pleasure - "I love you!" That couldn't be ... It was just sex, wasn't it? I was out of the role for a moment, and yet the situation excited me so much that I finally couldn't hold on to it. I poured myself into her dripping pussy, I pumped several hot spurts into her. Claudia looked into my eyes, a smile spread across her face, and when I slumped on her completely exhausted, she hugged me lovingly and gave me a kiss on the cheek. "Thank you, Thomas!" she whispered in my ear.

Claudia:

I could feel it for a brief moment. He was unsure, his eyes were wide open. But the next moment it broke out of him and he sprayed me, again and again his semen spurted into me until he collapsed out of breath on me. I was happy, overjoyed and put my arms around him. I wanted to feel his proximity and I knew he was the same. After seemingly endless minutes, I slowly turned and stood up. I took his hand in mine and pulled him up to me, put my hands on his shoulders and looked at him intently. "Stay with me tonight!" I begged him.

Thomas:

When we were reasonably strong again, Claudia pulled me up. I felt a little queasy. I had to go home, but what should the farewell be like But she didn't want to let me go, she wanted me to stay with her! I looked into her deep blue eyes and my mind just paused. I took Claudia in my arms, carried her to her bed and lay close to her, nestled close to her.

The End.

THE DELICATESSEN

Like every Friday, Professor Hallmaier entered the small but exclusive delicatessen in the middle of the pedestrian zone at the last minute. Nora gave him a businesslike smile as she locked the door behind him and flipped the OPEN / CLOSED sign.

"Getting late again ... Professor ...", stated Nora and went behind the counter. She knew she wouldn't get an answer, and she didn't care. The professor's lavish bills made up for the annoyance at his constant 'last minute coming'.

Professor Hallmaier nodded absentmindedly, pulled a crumpled note from his coat pocket and passed it over the counter. While Nora started to work through the list, the professor looked out the window. The icy December wind, mixed with a fine drizzle, made him shiver his shoulders even though it was warm.

Beth, the second owner of the delicatessen temple, came from behind where the private rooms were and greeted the professor with a handshake. She looked to see if she could still help her friend and co-owner, but Nora was already packing up the professor's purchases.

Together they said goodbye to the old man at the door, wished him a nice weekend and closed the shop door for the last time this week.

"Are we ready?" Asked Beth, smiling at her friend.

"Ready!" Grinned Nora, reaching for her friend's hand.

*

At the same time, Sven, Nora and Beth's 19-year-old apprentice, was in the locker room, which was in the back of the shop. He was sick of what was going to happen to him. And the worst part of it was that no matter how he turned or turned it, there was no way around the fact that Beth caught him wanking in the toilet. He took a cigarette out of the pack, held the tip in the flickering flame, and took a deep drag. He knew that his bosses didn't like to smoke. However, since he was still in the trial period and after the incident, he only expected his dismissal anyway. It didn't matter to the one glowing stalk.

*

Nora was sitting behind the desk, dealing with daily bills.

Beth was holding Sven's staff documents when there was a tentative knock on the door. She opened and saw Sven standing in front of her with a red head.

"Well, come on in then," she said, trying to sound stern, and nodded at the chair that stood in front of the massive desk.

Nora looked up briefly, but then went back to her numbers. She had to concentrate in order not to grin, or even to have to laugh.

Beth, who had celebrated her 50th a few weeks ago, sat half on the edge of the desk and flipped through the papers she was still holding. She let Sven braise in her own juice for five minutes. During this time she kept looking at her apprentice out of the corner of her eye. Sven was slim, medium-sized and slender. His soft facial features and the blonde curl that reached his shoulders gave him an almost feminine look. Beth thought briefly of the day when Sven entered the shop and asked for an apprenticeship. In fact, for a brief moment, she had thought he was a girl.

"You know why you're here?" Beth asked, looking sharply at Sven. He shifted nervously in his chair and nodded his head silently.

"And what should we do to you now? Can you tell us maybe?" Secretly she felt a little sorry for the poor guy. Sven was a treasure from an apprentice. Hardworking, helpful and willing. How willing, it would turn out in the next few minutes.

"What is it all about?", Nora interfered in mock ignorance.

Beth turned her upper body to the side and looked at her friend. With this movement, her costume skirt slipped a little and revealed the denser woven panties of her tights. Sven swallowed and stared between his boss's slightly opened thighs.

Beth, who had of course noticed this, gave Sven a punitive look. Then she turned back to Nora and said, "I caught our little apprentice sorcerer in the toilet this morning. And what I saw there ..." Beth shook her head. "I still can not believe it."

"I don't understand a word at all," said Nora, looking from Beth to Sven and back again. Then she got up, came around the desk and sat on the corner that was still free. Like Beth, she was wearing a costume, only that her bust size stretched the white blouse far more than was the case with her friend.

Sven didn't know where to look. His bosses, both of them over 50, played a not exactly small role in his wet dreams. And somehow the suspected start-up did not develop as he had feared. It didn't look like they were going to throw him out of his apprenticeship contract. A little glimmer of hope came up in Sven. He made up his mind to confess everything, to forgive and to promise holily that such a thing would never happen again. He looked up at Beth, took a deep breath and ...

... was interrupted by Beth.

"Just imagine, dear! When I passed the toilet this morning, I heard strange noises behind the door. I thought Sven had gotten sick and wanted to ask him if I could help him in any way. And what was it? There the little wanker sits on the toilet, has his tail in his hand and wags one of the palm! "

"Isn't it true!", Nora played the indignant.

"But if I tell you!" Beth exulted. She looked at the pile of misery sitting in front of her with ice-cold eyes and said: "Well, Sven! Show Nora how I caught you jerking off. And no false shame please! I've already seen your cock at full speed!"

Sven sat there with his jaw down and couldn't believe his ears. Such words from his boss's mouth? His head was about to burst and the first drops of sweat ran down his forehead and dripped from the tip of his `nose. And the worst of all: he had a murderous erection that pressed painfully against his pants. He looked imploringly at Beth, who smirked at him.

"Well, will it be soon?", She poisoned.

Sven thought about what he had planned. To his hot dreams and not least, of course, to his apprenticeship. As if in a trance, he fiddled with the sweaty fingers on the zipper of his jeans, pushed his underpants down and saw his cock stick out. Straight as a candle, the veins swollen thick, the glans fiery red, this is how he presented his masculinity to the two women.

"Whow!" Exclaimed Nora, wiping her lips with the tip of her tongue.

"Well," Beth commented triumphantly, "did I promise you too much?" Nora was still shaking her head speechless.

The blood roared in Sven's ears and it was difficult for him to grasp a clear thought. The whole situation was somewhat surreal, and he briefly considered whether he might not be lying in bed at home and dreaming of one of his wet dreams.

"Tell him to touch his handle," gasped Nora Beth.

"Didn't you hear?" Beth asked lurking, prompting her fingers to dance on her stocking knee.

Sven was afraid to touch his cock, which had grown a bit in the meantime. The velvety skin had pulled back a little and the chugging head was bare in the air. A lonely droplet of lust sparkled on the tip like a small diamond. Sven knew that if he touched his tail now, it would explode in no time. Beth seemed to suspect that too. She got up, took a small towel from the stack at the sink and threw it into Sven's lap. Then she sat down again, not without pushing up her skirt a lot. The moment Sven looked between her open thighs, his hand closed on his hot meat.

"Just look at our Sven," groaned Nora. She put a hand under her costume jacket and pressed it on her breasts. She watched intently as Sven's hand slid up and down.

Sven still couldn't believe what he was doing. But at least his mind was working so far that he no longer feared to be released. His jerking movements became more hectic as he stared at Beth under the skirt, believing she could see her cunt squeezing through a hint of panties. On the other side of the desk, Nora fondled her breasts.

And then suddenly everything happened very quickly. Sven's eyes had a glassy sheen, he pushed his thighs through and with a quick grip he held the towel so that the first splash went right through. It happened several times, even if the intensity became weaker from time to time. In the end he slumped in his chair and gasped for air.

When he was back to his senses, Nora and Beth were standing close to him. Business-wise, as if nothing had ever happened, Beth said: "Yes, my dear Sven. It was quite decent for the beginning. The best thing is to go back to the bathroom and freshen up. But hurry up! We want to go home too! " And after a little pause she added: "And don't forget: Monday morning at 10am. But on time, please!"

*

Sven's weekend had been hell. Torn between fear and hope, he fell into depression, then disappeared to his room in the blink of an eye and gave in to the pressure that had built up in his groin area. On Sunday evening he could hardly touch his best piece. It hurt, had turned blood red and still didn't want to rest.

*

On Monday morning, Sven had set three alarm clocks and, as a precaution, had taken an earlier train, he was half an hour earlier than necessary in the freezing cold in front of the store, waiting to be let in.

Nora and Beth were in a good mood when they got out of the car, greeted Sven and unlocked the shop door. Business-wise, the three immediately went to work, and because no word about what had happened passed over the lips of his bosses, Sven relaxed more and more by the hour. Escaping again with good skin, he thought to himself, and decided to buy a bouquet of flowers for Beth and Nora during lunch break.

*

The work was done, the shop was closed and Sven was putting on his everyday clothes in his little room when the door suddenly opened and Beth was standing in the frame.

Beth looked up and down at Sven, her gaze lingering longer than necessary on his bulging briefs. Sven immediately pulled his head between his shoulders and tried to cover his almost bare hands as best he could.

"We still wanted to thank you for the beautiful flowers," she said and came close to Sven.

"Um, yes, so ... I liked doing it," Sven stuttered.

"You know what women like. Don't you?" She flirted with her apprentice. Her fingertips slid over his bare thigh and for a split second touched the bulging bulge in his panties.

Sven fainted. He breathed the smell of his seductive boss and felt his panties get wet. Not that too, he thought in horror! But Beth, who had also noticed the misery, only licked her lips seductively.

"Do you actually know what Nora said when she saw the flowers on the desk?" Asked Beth. Sven shook his head so violently that his curly hair was flung wildly back and forth. "She said you definitely didn't have a girlfriend to give flowers to. I wonder if she was right about that?"

Sven couldn't keep it up. He slowly sank down on the little bench and looked embarrassed at the floor at his feet.

The answer was enough for Beth. "Poor boy!" She said softly, stroking the back of her hand on his cheek. Then she put both hands on his head and pressed him against her lap. Sven felt her heat and in a fit of despair he wrapped his arms around Beth's waist and held her tightly. After a minute or two he realized that his hands were on his boss's buttocks and he let go of her, startled. Instead of the expected thunderstorm, Beth put her hand under Sven's chin. She raised his face and said softly, "Nora and I could use your help. Do you have time on Saturday?" Sven looked his boss in the eye and nodded silently. "That's fine. Around 3pm? You know where we live."

*

On Tuesday after business hours, Sven was stowing some boxes in the fridge when Nora entered the room with a fruit staircase. Sven eagerly took the load off her and put it on the shelf. When he turned again, he hit Nora, who was now a step closer to him.

"I heard you are coming to see us on Saturday?" She whispered in a voice that Sven immediately shot in the abdomen.

"Um, yes, gladly!", Sven nodded uncertainly and tried to get to her breasts. Until the shelf in his back prevented another escape.

"You know that you were very lucky? Normally you don't let something like that happen to an apprentice."

Sven nodded in concern. He was about to take a breath to apologize again when Nora cut him off.

"I can well imagine what it's like. No girlfriend ... the hormones go crazy ... it makes you nonsense!" She looked into Sven's face, which was slowly growing in color. "Don't be so shy! Now you have us!" And with a smile, she added: "It might not be bad if you gave your wand some rest until Saturday. It won't be your damage!"

Sven felt her hand cautiously pressing against his crotch and it was as if she was burning a hole in his pants from the sheer heat.

*

Saturday afternoon, at 3 p.m., Sven rang at Beth's apartment door. He held the lush bouquet of flowers in front of him like a shield when the door opened and Nora smiled brightly.

"Come in," she asked, taking the flower greeting from him. Sven looked around and was amazed. The apartment was spacious and modern. A lot of white leather and chrome dominated, but the two women still managed to give the rooms a feminine touch. Later that evening, Sven was told that Beth and Nora had bought the two adjoining apartments. Although each of them lived in one of the apartments, a removed wall made it easy to switch back and forth.

Sven was sitting at the glass coffee table, holding his second cocktail. The unusual mixture made him a little more relaxed, even if he still couldn't make sense of the invitation. Which is exactly where they need my help, he thought as Beth and Nora rose and apologized for a moment. Sven didn't dare to get up to look around the room more closely, but he let his gaze wander and marveled at the view through the large picture window.

A rustle behind him wrenched him out of his reverie. The two women had entered the living room and were taking their old places again. Sven's eyes grew bigger and bigger. His bosses had changed and were now wearing lavender, slightly shimmering house suits, which they had loosely fastened at the front with a belt made of fabric. The excess of bare legs made Sven sweat a lot. Of course, he had no idea that Beth had turned the thermostat up a bit. When Nora leaned over to hand him a cigarette and he could look into her deep cleavage for a brief moment, it finally became too tight for Sven's tail in the fashionable jeans. He struggled restlessly on the white leather armchair, trying to relieve himself.

While Beth and Nora kept their conversation with Sven as businesslike as possible, at the same time they tried to spice up Sven with clumsy movements and provoked contortions. Which they did extremely well. Until Nora got up, mixed another cocktail at the bar and then approached the armchair in which Sven was sitting. Kneeling on the floor, she put her hands on Sven's knee and looked up at him.

"Do you remember what you promised us?" Asked Nora, stroking Sven's thigh with her hand.

Sven looked down at his boss and nodded. When he had been thinking about what the two women wanted from him over the past few days, he naturally had the idea that they might have an erotic interest in him. However, he had always immediately rejected this thought.

Sven looked shyly into Nora's eyes and said in a low voice: "I had promised to make up for my impropriety."

"Oh what ... impropriety ... There was never any talk of that," Beth interfered from further back. She rested one foot on the edge of the glass table and Sven saw her snow-white panties flash for a moment.

"What Beth wants to say," chuckled Nora in the most beautiful little girl's voice, "you really messed her up with your appearance." And a bit more conspiratorial: "She doesn't speak of anything else!"

"What is there to whisper about?" Insisted Beth, smiling. She got up and sat on the other side of Sven's armchair. "What Nora REALLY wants to say is that she's terribly jealous. She just doesn't allow me what I've seen!"

"Not at all!" Exclaimed Nora, but it didn't sound particularly convincing.

Sven looked to the left, then to the right. His bosses at his feet?!? Did they courtship about him?!? The rustle in his ears for a brief moment submerged all other noises.

"I need another drink! And I need a cigarette too!" Sven said throatily. And for the first time, his voice sounded like a man's.

The two women at Sven's feet behaved more and more. And because they were much closer to the underfloor heating than Sven, their plan to heat Sven vigorously came back to them as a boomerang. They loosened the belts of their coats and Sven caught more than a look at her seductive cleavage. Beth, with a much smaller bust than Nora, wore a snow-white half-cup bra that showed only a crescent-shaped sickle from her large areolas. Nora, on the other hand, wore a white, mid-high bustier with firm cups. Both women had a handsome figure, even though they hadn't been panting for the supposed beauty ideal for a long time.

Sven was slowly but surely feeling more comfortable. His alcohol level overshadowed his shyness, and it was clear to him that nothing bad would happen to him that evening. He took turns looking down at Beth and Nora, and felt like the King himself. And so Nora's almost hysterical request: "We want to see your cock now", no longer really upset.

Slowly, subliminally aware of his power, he pulled the zipper of his jeans in slow motion. His bosses' eyes grew bigger and bigger. They nervously fiddled with their fabric belts and fanned air into the cleavage with their flat hands. Sven had continued to work ahead. One more grip, then the part of him was honored with loud "Ohs" and "Ahs", the bulging, and glowing dark red at the tip, perpendicular to it.

"Touch him!" Gasped Nora as Beth licked her lips.

Sven giggled as his hand wrapped around the chugging flesh. Slowly he pulled back the velvet skin and a first drop of longing appeared at the top.

"It's really as big as you said," Nora said to Beth.

"I tell you," Beth replied, rubbing the inside of Sven's thigh with her hand.

Nora stared at Sven's tail and his half-hearted hand movements. "Now jerk off!" She hissed violently at her apprentice. "Come on, finally!"

For a brief moment Sven realized what he was doing here. But uninhibited by the cocktails, and long ago caught up in his own lust, he wiped his thoughts aside and accelerated his hand movements.

It didn't take long for Sven to feel his scrotum contract. He looked into the gaping faces of the two women at his feet and saw their greed in them. Beth was still massaging his thighs as Nora tore apart the top of her house suit and pulled the heavy breasts out of her cups. Her warts were erect and she rolled them back and forth between thumb and forefinger.

It was definitely too much for Sven. His fist flew up and down faster and faster, and at the last moment he saw Beth reach for her empty cocktail glass and hold it in front of the tip of his tail. With several powerful, and above all productive splashes, he filled the glass with his creamy sperm. Then he slumped in his chair, gasping for air on the dry.

*

Half an hour later, Beth and Nora took their apprentice to the door. Sven smiled a little tormentedly, and as if in a trance he took the hundred that Beth gave him with a blink of an eye.

"Taxi money!" She said with a smile.

Then the door closed behind him and he was left alone with an experience that would take his newly awakened sex life in a completely different, unexpected direction.

*

Beth and Nora sat opposite and smoked.

"That was good!", Nora grinned at her friend.

"I told you!" Answered Beth. "Much better than the last one!"

"Yes, I agree!"

After a while, pondering their thoughts, Beth said, "We could invite Simone next time?"

"Simone is an old, spoiled, loud and vulgar cow!" Replied Nora in the chest tone of conviction.

"Right!" Beth attested. "That's why it suits us so well!"

Both women cackled until their eyes caught on the cocktail glass filled by Sven.

"What are we going to do with it now?" Asked Nora hypocritically.

"Cold sperm is yuck!" Beth grimaced.

"What do we have a microwave for?" Grinned Nora Beth like a honey cake horse.

On the way to the kitchen, Beth laughed and smacked the friend next to her on the buttocks.

"And YOU say Simone was spoiled?!?"

*

On Monday, Sven was standing in the freezing cold outside the shop just before eight, waiting for his bosses. He was excited and a little unsure of how they would behave towards him, but no longer worried that something bad would happen to him. The almost lovingly kicked out on Saturday and the crackling hundreds in his breast pocket spoke a different language.

Beth and Nora got out of their car and Sven saw their good mood at first sight.

"Well? Fit again?" Beth asked suggestively, and Nora couldn't help giggling.

"Let the poor boy wake up first," she rebuked her friend. "Of course he's fit! Isn't it Sven?"

Sven swallowed, stammered: "Klaro", and hurried to close the shop door behind him.

A few minutes later, Sven had moved and made his way to the cold room. Once there, he saw Nora, who was examining some of the delicate fruits before they went on sale again. Sven stacked the controlled stairs on a small trolley, which he would later push into the elevator. When they stood back to back, Sven felt Nora's downside pressing against his behind. Sven immediately realized that this had not happened by chance when the contact became more intense. Undaunted, Nora pressed her very best against Sven. He enjoyed it for a while, but then turned and looked at the bulging rear part, which charmingly rounded off the peach-colored costume skirt. Nora stretched, looked over her shoulder, and looked at Sven.

"Oops ..." she grinned cheekily before going back to work.

Monday was the weakest day of the week, so Sven was busy pushing cans a few millimeters to the right on a shelf and then pushing them back to the left once they got to the end. He did so with such fervor that he only noticed Nora's call the third time.

"Sven. Can you please go to the office and get the new price tags?"

Sven nodded to Nora, adjusted the last can and went back. He knocked on the door to the office and the next moment he opened it without being asked. Just as he was used to. But what he saw then left him speechless.

Beth stood in the middle of the room with her skirt gathered. In one hand the loose straps, in the other the lace-embellished edge of her stocking. Sven stood there stiff for a moment, staring openly at Beth. Or more precisely: he stared at the naked, white meat between his skirt and stocking.

"Oh, sorry!" He stammered. "I'll be right back!"

"Well, don't be shy, young man," Beth said, her voice not at all angry. "What did you want?"

"Um, yes. Nora is sending me the new price tags," Sven said quietly and just couldn't look away.

"They're over there," Beth replied, looking over to a small shelf. "Damn it!" She cursed as the straps slipped through her fingers again.

Sven hastily reached for the box and hurriedly left the office.

Beth routinely fastened her straps and sat on her office chair. "We'll cook you really soft this week," Beth murmured softly, to correct herself immediately: "No. Not soft. Al dente!"

Sven Nora gave the box with shining red ears, then devoted himself again to his cans.

Nora, however, put away the price tags, which she could not use anyway. But she was thievingly pleased that the timing with Beth had apparently worked perfectly.

Sven noticed after work that Sven's bosses were serious about the final seduction of her apprentice. Beth had sent him for a ladder because she wanted to get something from the top shelf. Sven offered to do it for her, but Beth gallantly blocked him off.

"Just hold on to the ladder," she said, climbing the stairs. Standing on the last step, she started looking for something specific in a box.

Sven stood close to the ladder and his hands clung to the two bars. Securing himself, he looked first to the left, then to the right. Nora was nowhere to be seen. Taking all her courage together, Sven looked up. What he saw made his wildest hopes look pale. He had known that his boss was wearing stockings since he had surprised Beth that morning. That he now saw her bare cheeks flashing under her skirt almost knocked him out of his shoes.

Beth stretched and stretched, spreading her feet as far as the ladder allowed, and squeezing her butt out that it was a pleasure. She thought of her panties, which were on her desk, and Nora, who was sitting in front of the small monitor of the surveillance camera at that moment and could not keep her hands still.

"Ah, there it is," she said aloud, taking something out of the box. She looked down at Sven, who just managed to look at her with a harmless face. "Are you still taking the ladder away? And then you're going to be finishing work. Yes?", She fluted and floated away like a goddess.

*

Sven saw a lot of bare meat this week and his hormone levels rose to scary heights. However, in an almost masochistic manner, he did nothing to change this. He secretly hoped his bosses would fix it.

Finally, on Friday after closing time, the time had come. Sven had changed in his little room, and before he went home he checked the office. Beth was sitting on the couch, leafing through a magazine. She had stripped off her pumps, put her stockings on the table and Sven saw her red-painted toenails shimmering through the fine nylon. Beth looked up from her reading and smiled kindly at her apprentice.

Nora was sitting behind the desk and her fingers flicked across the computer keyboard. When she saw Sven standing in the door frame, she waved him over with her hand. Sven went up to her and saw that she had opened the top buttons of her blouse. Her breasts bulged almost out of the cups, and Sven couldn't help but stare into her neckline.

And then finally Nora's redeeming question: "Do you have any plans for tomorrow after the shop closes?"

Sven couldn't help but smile when he replied truthfully, "No. I have no plans for tomorrow."

"But that's a good thing," hypocritized Beth from the background. In truth, of course, the two women had hoped that Sven would keep the weekend free, as Sven had expected to be invited again. "We were hoping we could make ourselves comfortable," continued Beth.

"I really like to come," said Sven. When he realized how ambiguous his answer had been, his ears began to glow.

"Yes. Do that," replied Nora and Beth and released Sven. No sooner was the two of them burst out of the door.

"The boy is worth gold!" Said Beth.

"That's right. It's really cute!"

*

Punctually on the late Saturday afternoon, Sven rang the doorbell on Beth's apartment door. It took a while, then the door opened and Nora motioned Sven inside.

"The food has just been finished," she said and thankfully took the bouquet from Sven. She hooked on his arm and led him into the kitchen with the large dining area.

Sven's enthusiasm that he had planned to be a little more relaxed for the evening was immediately dampened when he saw an unknown woman sitting at the table.

"May I introduce Simone to you? She is a good friend of ours."

When Nora saw Sven's petrified look, she added with a smile: "You don't have to be afraid of her. Simone knows about it and is really looking forward to you."

That was exactly what Sven feared. But politely as he was, he shook hands with Simone and wished her a nice day.

Meanwhile, Nora had a tray with four champagne flutes in her hand.

"Are you coming too?", She said to Beth, who did the last handles in the kitchen.

"Have a nice evening!" Said Nora, holding up her glass.

"Have a nice evening," said the others, and Sven stole a glance over at Simone. She was significantly older than his bosses, but still had an appealing figure and a pleasant smile. When she spoke to Sven for the first time, he winced.

"You mustn't resent Simone!" Explains Beth Sven. Her husband is hard of hearing, which is why she always screams.

"That's not true at all!" Said Simone in a loud voice.

The table was already set, and while Nora and Beth put the meat platter, the bowls of potatoes, vegetables, and salad on the table, Sven realized for the first time that all the women in white dressing gowns were sitting at the table. After the welcome sparkling wine there was wine and Sven tipped his first glass down in one go. He had seen three opened bottles on a small side table, and he could guess what they were for. No sooner had he put his glass down than Beth refilled it.

After the meal, the women quickly cleared the table. Sven took the liberty, after a bottle of wine he had become much more courageous to take a small tour of the apartment. He already knew the guest toilet, but the bathroom did offer some surprises. Two washstands, and the shelves filled with innumerable tubes and jars testified to more than one user. Sven was no longer surprised that he found a wide double bed in the bedroom.

"Curious?" Heard Sven Nora's voice behind her and slowly turned around.

"You live together ...?"

"Sometimes more, sometimes less", laughed Nora and pressed against Sven.

Sven felt Nora's hand slowly sliding into his crotch. At the same time, she put the other hand behind his head and pulled him close. Sven could hardly believe it when her soft lips pressed against his mouth and he felt the tip of her tongue between his lips. Sven wrapped his arms and Nora and pulled her close.

Unfortunately at that moment Beth came into the bedroom and disturbed them.

"Oh, here you are!", She said laughing and put a hand on Nora's shoulder. "But that's not fair of you, dear! We also want to have fun!"

"Too bad!" Whispered Nora Sven with a wink.

In the meantime the four had emptied another bottle and the mood reached its peak. The three girls were sitting side by side on the sofa when Sven came out of the toilet.

"Come to us, young man," roared Simone, and Sven, who had still not got used to her loud organ, winced. But he answered her call and built himself up in front of the phalanx of femininity.

"The two of them," said Simone, looking left and right, "have told me real miracles about you." Then she reached behind Sven's belt, pulled him the last bit, and, faster than Sven noticed, she had opened his belt buckle and pulled down the zipper. His pants were on his knees with a single jerk, and the fact that Simone had caught his underpants showed a certain routine in these matters.

"Whow!" She exclaimed as Sven's best piece jumped outside. "But the girls didn't promise me too much," she said, licking her lips with relish. She looked up and nodded encouragingly to Sven. "Now grab the syringe and fling it back and forth properly!"

Sven first had to process what Simone wanted from him, because he was not used to such coarse sayings from Beth and Nora. But he also knew why he was here, so he put his hand around his best piece and slowly pushed the foreskin back and forth. Simone looked at it for a while, then nudged Beth, whose hand had sneaked into her dressing gown and was rhythmically lifting the fabric.

"The boy jerks like he's going to sleep," she blasphemed.

But Beth didn't react at all, but stared at Sven's cock. Simone's eyes fell on Nora, who was tugging at her nipples behind the fabric of her fluffy coat.

"Why don't you tell me something ..." roared Simone. Nora glared at Simone, then sighed unmistakably. Simone shook her head.

"Well how is the wanker going to get going when you're sitting like monastery students? You have to offer the guy something!"

With these words, she tore open the belt of her dressing gown and showed Sven that she didn't really care about underwear.

"You're amazed, aren't you?" She shouted at Sven while opening her thighs. "Take a close look! Very best fuck meat ... and that at the age of 62!"

Everything started to spin in Sven's head. He had never seen anything like it. And the best: The old woman was right, because her figure was really still in top shape. That her breasts hung down like heavy dumplings and the thick, dark brown tips almost touched the belly button did not disturb the overall impression. On the contrary, the opposite was the case. Sven's fist shifted back and forth with a monkey tooth, which Simone commented with: "Well, go!" She tugged her labia with both hands, then pulled them apart until they formed a funnel. "Well you horny stallion ... Where do you want to squirt your goo?", She spurred Sven on. "On my nice tits, am I right?" Simone let her labia flit back and lifted her soft breasts with both hands. These were now presented like large pancakes in front of Sven, who had his severe problems with the overstimulation and could no longer control himself. In several powerful bursts, he discharged himself and sprayed his sperm on Simone's breasts. When he could think clearly again, he saw Simone holding her breasts under Nora's eyes, then Beth's. "Do you see girls that?", She called completely unnecessarily. "That's how you do it!" Then she started to spread Sven's sperm over her breasts and massage it conscientiously. In several powerful bursts, he discharged himself and sprayed his sperm on Simone's breasts. When he could think clearly again, he saw Simone holding her breasts under Nora's eyes, then Beth's. "Do you see girls that?", She called completely unnecessarily. "That's how you do it!" Then she started to spread Sven's sperm over her breasts and massage it conscientiously. In several powerful bursts, he discharged himself and sprayed his sperm on Simone's breasts. When he could think clearly again, he saw Simone holding her breasts under Nora's eyes, then Beth's. "Do you see girls that?", She called completely unnecessarily. "That's how you do it!" Then she started to spread Sven's sperm over her breasts and massage it conscientiously.

An hour later the round was broken up. Beth had just slipped the obligatory taxi hundreds for Sven when Simone came and hung herself in Sven's arm without being asked. She accompanied him to the door and it didn't seem to bother her at all that her dressing gown gaped wide and her naked body was visible.

"You were really top class!" She whispered, and Sven was surprised that there was something else, nice, to say than obscenities screaming around. As she pushed Sven through the door, she briefly put her hand in his jacket pocket.

On the way to the bus stop, Sven looked curiously at what she had slipped into him. It was another banknote, and Sven whistled with approval.

*

Half a year had passed and Sven had come to terms with getting the three women into the finals only through their own efforts.

On the one hand he didn't like it, on the other hand he was really well. And he would do the devil to endanger that. After passing his journeyman's examination, he got a contract that was impressive. In the meantime, he drove a chic sports car and was already looking around for a new apartment.

*

The Christmas season was over, as was the turn of the year, and somewhat calmer times were returning to Beth and Nora's deli.

*

It all started with Beth inviting him for Sunday afternoon. That was unusual because until now he was only allowed to come to them on Saturday. Beth didn't explain this to Sven, but at least betrayed so much that Simone wouldn't come. Sven could live with that, because he had still not got used to this loud and ordinary person. Beth winked at him as she correctly interpreted his face.

"Don't be too early, Sven. We have prepared a really big surprise for you!" With these words, they released Sven into the weekend.

*

The door opened and in front of Sven stood a woman who was completely alien to him. Sven hastily looked at the doorbell again: No! He was right!

"Now come in! Or do you want to take root out there?" The stranger snapped at Sven and looked at him with her turquoise eyes.

"Oh, sorry," stammered Sven, who had suddenly lost all the coolness that he had built up in the past few months.

"Oh, there you are," Beth released him from the predicament he was in. "I see you've already met Tamara."

"Yes ...", stammered Sven and let Beth pull her into the living room.

A little later the four sat in the comfortable armchairs of the seating group and drank cocktails that Nora had mixed. Beth and Nora wore their fluffy dressing gowns as usual.

The new one, however, was clearly out of the ordinary. Sven estimated her to be in her mid-20s. She was tall, certainly as tall as he was. Her clothes consisted of black, opaque tights that shimmered metallic in the light of the lamps. She was wearing a very tight black leather mini skirt. Under her likewise black wool sweater with silver-colored lurex threads, a considerable bust bulged. Her ankle boots with ridiculously high heels were the same color as her blood-red varnished fingernails. The frame of her modern glasses was a slightly darker red, and her long, night-black hair was artfully pinned up. Tamara's voice was pleasantly soft and smoky timbre. Every word she said seemed thoughtful, the sentences short and sweet. In short: Sven was blown away,

And her questions increasingly troubled Sven. When Tamara asked him, for example, why he would masturbate in front of his bosses, he got a crimson head and pressed around. But Tamara did not give up, literally feasted on his shyness. It was only too obvious that she was enjoying his helplessness.

"So if he can't speak, then he should come here," she commanded Sven to himself.

Sven got up as if in a trance, approached her with tentative steps and stopped about a meter in front of her. Tamara slid her foot between his thighs and pressed the fine leather firmly into his crotch. Although Sven was more than embarrassed, he instantly got a murderous erection, which of course was not hidden from the women. Nora, Beth, and Tamara discussed the phenomenon as if they were talking about the weather, and Sven wanted to sink into the ground. Still, he couldn't take his eyes off Tamara, whose female arrogance magically attracted him. And so he did not notice at first how Nora approached him from behind and opened his belt with nimble hands. He pulled the jeans and his underpants down to his knees and laughed.

"That explains why there is no blood left in the head," Tamara smiled indulgently, and bent her head to the left and right so that she could look at Sven's splendid specimen from all sides.

"But you don't leave the boy with good hair?" Beth said censely and now got up as well and approached Sven.

"Why? I think he is very cute!" Said Tamara, who meanwhile rocked Sven's tail with his toe. "Doesn't he want to show us what he can do with it?", She asked lurking and looked at Sven sharply.

And Sven did what he had done many times before. Slowly, like in slow motion, he started massaging his cock. Tamara was sitting in front of him, his bosses were kneeling to his left and right, staring at his acorn, which disappeared into his fist, reappeared, disappeared and became visible again.

Tamara looked at it bored for a few minutes, then her hand shot forward. The thumb and forefinger wrapped around his scrotum as a ring while she carefully scratched his testicle with the pinky nail.

Sven was shocked! He was touched for the first time during his performance, and the how and who made him sway for a brief moment. Without stopping in what he was doing, he stared at Tamara, who mocked her grip.

"If you spit on me little piglet, you will never forget that in your life!" Said Tamara in a soft voice, which at that moment did not match her steel-hard look.

But Sven was past the point where he could have prevented worse. The tugging on his scrotum had made him so horny that only a few strokes were missing, and he exploded like never before. When he saw splashes of splash from his tail and ruin Tamara's sweater, he knew this was his death sentence.

Guiltily, he pulled his head between his shoulders as Tamara got up and stood close to him. With both hands she pulled the smeared sweater over her head and pressed it to Sven's chest.

"Take it to the bathroom!" Tamara whispered dangerously softly. Sven, however, only stared at her bare breasts, which stood firm and firm against her. "Yes, do you like them?", She asked and sat back in her chair as she was.

Sven nodded before turning and going to the bathroom. He heard the women laughing behind him, and it was more than embarrassing. In the bathroom he threw the sweater in the laundry basket and sat on the edge of the bathtub. He knew he messed everything up. And of all people with whom he had fallen head over heels in love ...

*

epilogue

*

Many years have passed since then and nothing is as it was.

Nora suffered a stroke from which she never really recovered. Paralyzed from the waist down and mentally confused, she relies on outside help.

Beth has left the deli and is taking care of her friend with sacrifice. She washes her, she feeds her, and she reads it to her from the newspaper every morning, even though she knows that Nora understands none of this. But Nora's smile is enough for Beth.

After the death of her husband, Simone sold the house in which she lived with her husband for over 30 years. From the proceeds she bought into a 'assisted living project'. She quickly became friends with the other women on her floor. However, some of the seniors complain that Simone is too loud ... and terribly vulgar!

Tamara, by the way, she is Beth's daughter, has taken over her mother's delicatessen. However, she does not work there, but only occasionally checks that everything is in order. Her dominatrix studio on the other side of the city is flourishing and recently she has shared her work with another dominatrix.

Sven is now married. With Tamara. During the day, he conscientiously runs the delicatessen to lie at his wife's feet in the truest sense of the word. Tamara consequently punishes mistakes in the store or in the household, for which he is also responsible, with the cane. Sven loves his wife more than anything, and his greatest wish is to sleep with her once, as husband and wife usually do. However, this prevents a chastity belt, which Tamara had made especially for Sven. So far, Sven has only been able to provide relief with her permission and before her eyes.

And then came the day Tamara wanted to have a child from Sven. But this also went differently than Sven hoped for. After all, she allowed him to push the fully injected condom deep into her cunt.

The End.

Anniversary

It felt as if she had been standing in this completely dark room for hours. With her face to the wall, hands and feet, like on a St. Andrew's cross, chained and completely naked, they had been left here alone. Had Joan persuaded herself to be brave by saying:

"He doesn't forget me. He is somewhere in the dark and is probably amused by his stupid slave who is slowly getting scared ..."

so the panic had grown into the immeasurable.

The room was very warm, even the stone wall to which it was attached, and little beads of sweat began to run down her body. They tickled her, especially those looking down the side of her body. As far as she could, she jerked her body to shake it off. Except for the clink of the chains and her own breath, she could hear no sound.

Then a door or passage opened far away to her left and someone came near her. Without saying a word, the person began to cleanse their body with a soft sponge and lukewarm water. Joan felt the sponge reduce the heat on the back of her neck, how it slid gently over her shoulders, shoulder blades and narrow back. She took a deep breath, because the feeling was extremely pleasant, apart from the additional, fresh scent of flowers that was now spreading around her. If she had been a cat, she would have purred for sure now.

When the sponge moved between her thighs, a shiver of pleasure swept over her and she moved her pelvis backwards. But that turned out to be a mistake, because she got a good slap on the butt.

"Ouch!" It escaped her and her buttock burned again. So she tried to show no reaction, while the soft, moist ball refreshed her labia and finally slid between them. Joan had to pull herself together so as not to escape a slight sigh from her lips to have.

their legs were able to enjoy the refreshment and Joan's spirits returned gloriously.

Then her head was pulled back by the hair and the cool water was spread over her face. With slight pressure against her chest she was shown to detach herself from the wall and she followed. Then her breast was refreshed and pampered in the most gentle and sensual way. She knew she couldn't let herself go and moan softly, which she would have loved to do now. So she opened her lips and let the resulting lust noiselessly escape. For long, far too long, the sponge material rubbed and irritated her feminine attributes, paying increased attention to Joan's pronounced nipples at the end. She found it increasingly difficult to control both her sounds and her body movements.

"I can do it! I will be obedient, "she repeated internally like a mantra.

But when a clearly female hand took hold of her breast, which was already refreshed

and pressed her big hard nipple tightly , it was too much. " Hmmmmm "she moaned and squeezed her breast towards the touch.

For a short time, both hand and sponge caresses continued, while Joan forgot the fear of punishment and groaned again and again. These feelings were too beautiful not to be enjoyed with every pore in the body.

Then the hand came loose and the sponge moved across her ribs, flat stomach and hips to her venus mound. Just as she was preparing to feel the pleasure of touching her clit the next second, the "freshener" stopped and began circular movements millimeters from the point that longed for it so much. Joan's body took on a life of its own and began to move within the tight bondage, hoping that she could overcome the remaining millimeter herself.

The only thing she could get was a hard pat on her ass. The soft something on her abdomen, however, had accomplished considerably more. Joan was more than excited, she had become extremely horny. She clearly felt the moisture in her vagina and when she was refreshed and cleaned there it was no longer possible for her to endure the gentle stimuli without a slight sigh.

Then her legs were cared for at the front and finally the pleasant interlude ended just as suddenly as it had started.

Frustrated and very excited, she huddled against the stone wall and tried to increase or at least maintain the stimulus by pressing her venus hill against the wall. She didn't succeed.

An eternity later, the door opened again. This time, several men entered the room, as she recognized by the heavy steps. She was touched again. But this time without a delicate object. This time it was possessive men's hands that squeezed and kneaded their butts, opened their cheeks and played at their entrance. More hands grabbed her breasts to play with, lift her up, torture her nipples with her fingers, and finally activate every single cell in her body. Joan's excitement was back to boiling in no time. And if she now turned and moved her body, moaned and made low sounds of pain, there would be no punishment. The men drove them to lustful heights.

Just when she thought that the moment of wonderful relaxation was at hand, all touches stopped and the men loosened their bonds. With gentle but consistent movements, they led Joan towards the light ....

Just before they were supposed to go through the opening, the men gave her the opportunity for a moment to get her eyes used to the bright light. When she could open her eyes normally, Joan realized that she had been led through the building her master had taken her to hours ago.

The men took her arms and led them through the door. She felt the sun on her skin and the light wind that gave her bare skin goosebumps. Finally she was standing in the middle of the very spacious courtyard and when she was turned around she realized that she was facing a large grandstand. She was startled. What should happen to her? What had her master planned? Desperately, she scanned the bleachers to find his face, to finally get at least some security from his presence. However, she did not find him and despaired.

"He left me alone," it shot through her head. "What kind of people are they in the stands and which men had just touched their whole bodies and could even give them pleasure?"

She would have just liked to vanish. But that was not possible because the men next to her held her. She couldn't even hide her nudity because they were holding her hands away from her and they were now slowly turning around on their own axis as if they wanted to show off their nakedness. Joan tried to pull away, but the hands on her arms gripped all the more tightly. She was standing with her back to the stands as one of the men around her grabbed her hair and slowly pulled her head forward and downward. Joan was forced to give in and seconds later she was aware that she was now openly presenting her most intimate places to everyone in the stands. Then finally ....

"Look at them. There stands in her absolutely natural beauty the woman who conquers my heart and gives my body and soul with her unlimited humility and obedience every second of my life in an indescribable way every pleasure that I just desire. "

The voice of her master! Joan could have screamed with happiness, he hadn't left her alone! How could she have doubted him ....

The men turned her around and she saw him approaching, wearing the white tuxedo that she wore so much loved him because he was a wonderful contrast to his sun-tanned skin and dark hair. He usually only wore his skin underneath, she knew that. Was it the same today?

The applause to speak to her master had died down and it was standing a few meters in front of her when the men released her. She wanted to throw himself into his arms when he raised his hand and brought it to a standstill.

"How do you greet your master's beloved beauty?" He asked without feeling.

Joan dropped to her knees and opened her legs as far as she could. Then she put her hands behind her back, each with her elbow Arms took hold, her lips were slightly open and her arms were pushed a little more into the foreground by the arms folded behind her back.

Her mind was racing. Would he greet her today as he usually did in her apartment? Would he take her hard cock deep down her throat in a slow push? He knew that she still had that gag reflex, though less now. And especially today and in front of all these people, she couldn't disappoint him ...

He came closer and closer. Yes, and he opened his pants under which he wasn't wearing any underwear. His hard giver of joy jumped out and was now right in front of her face. Joan knew what was expected of her. She opened her mouth as far as possible and he gently pushed his penis in. At first it was only the tip that she liked so much and immediately played around with her tongue. After a while he continued to penetrate her. Joan did what he had taught her in many exercises, sometimes using the whip. She tried to relax her throat as much as possible.

His cock continued to slide into her and she almost cheered with joy when she felt no gag reflex. She took it deeper and deeper in her mouth and enclosed it with her lips. With pride, she slowly began to move her head back and forth.

If he had only recently used some force to push her head closer to his abdomen, today he had his arms crossed over his chest and was spoiled by her.

Joan's movements became faster. Every now and then she even let it slip out of her mouth so that she could breathe for a moment. Then again she eagerly devoured his manhood. And again she felt how her lust increased, how her horny cunt - that is what she called her when he had really wet her - opened and closed in anticipation of the possible enjoyment of this gem a little later. She blew him with all the means at her disposal, even carefully inserting her teeth to give him an additional charm. Her master started to moan and Joan was delighted.

Then she felt how he started to twitch and in anticipation of his love juice her abdomen also started to cramp more wildly. Suddenly he pulled it completely out of her mouth and since she hadn't expected it she smacked loudly. The audience laughed.

Her master reached under her chin and motioned for her to stand up. She followed. When she stood he turned her around and with gentle pressure on her neck he showed her that she should lean forward.

"Take your hands for help as you have learned," he ordered.

Joan loosened her hands from her back, leaned forward, and wrapped her arms around her lower legs. Her master gripped her hips to support her while his mighty Pleasure tool slid deep into her wet crack now, and Joan cried out in delight.

He paused for a moment, sunk into it.

"Are you ready?" He asked.

"Yes sir, more than ever. Aaaaaaaaah!" she literally shouted back.

While she was still answering, he had started to fuck her hard, deep and fast. He knew that it would cause her to orgasm in seconds and she knew that he intended THAT.

She fidgeted and screamed, she begged him to fuck her further, deeper, harder ... And he did her every favor and then she screamed, long, bright and piercing ...

"Aaaaaaaaiiiiiiiiiieeeeeeeeee"

Her orgasm shook her body and again and again her vaginal muscles contracted to relax and then again powerfully cramp. Before the eyes of the audience, she surrendered to her master, her lover, the content of her life with every fiber of her body and let him do whatever he wanted. And he wanted ...

.... to come! Inject deep into it and thereby bring it to another climax.

Now he also screamed his lust and Joan felt clearly how her abdomen absorbed his delicious juice and actually gave her the pleasure of another highlight.

His movements became gentler and slowly both came back down to earth.

He grabbed his beloved slave's hair and raised her up. Then he turned her to the bleachers and ordered her to open her thighs wide. Joan obeyed and felt his juice begin to drip from her vagina. The audience applauded again. He grabbed her shoulders and turned her to face him. Then he looked deep into her eyes. "Beloved slave J." he began and continued: "Today you belong to me for a whole year to the day and today you showed me and the friends here how wonderful it is for me and for yourself."

Joan could only nod.

"So I ask you here and now: Slave J. do you want to spend your entire life with me and be my beloved wife as Joan?"

Joan had tears in her eyes when she happily replied,

"Yes, sir. I want that as your slave, as your wife and as your partner in all situations in which you need it. "

Under the applause of the spectators, both sank in an endless kiss.

Later the men who led them out brought a splendid short Dress and Joan slipped in. Underwear was not allowed in his presence anyway and right now it was her own wish to feel the gentle breath of the wind on her hot crevice with every step she took now ...

The End.

General and princess

The costume party

It will finally take place next weekend: The hottest costume festival in the whole city. Horny in the truest sense of the word! I have never participated and the little that I know has been told or circulated as a rumor among friends. Getting an invitation is pretty much out of the question unless you have a friend who is the host's daughter. Carmen, my friend, has never been allowed to participate, her parents have always forbidden it, which of course makes the whole thing much more mysterious and of course much more exciting. By chance, Carmen saw the invitation list on her father's secretary's PC and, when the secretary was out of the room, quickly put my name and address on the list. Today my invitation came in the mail. With luck, I intercepted the mail and put the letter aside. My feeling whispered to me that it would be better if dad and mom didn't know about it.

For the uninitiated, I think that was a bit much and a bit of a mess, which I have reported so far, so slowly from the beginning:

My name is Juliane, in my school in Hamburg most people call me "Jule". Carmen is my best Your parents are rich, very rich, but Carmen is still super OK, not a bit conceited. My dad knows Carmen's parents, who have something to do with one another.

Some time ago, my parents were invited to dinner there, my mom was speechless - and that means something. Carmen's parents live in Blankenese, she says in a huge house, more like a palace. You can't see anything from the street except a wall and a park behind it.

A very private costume party takes place in this sharp house every year. Nobody knows anything about it, but the party always ends in a wild orgy. The word orgy alone stimulates my imagination. It sounds wicked, forbidden and incredibly exciting. Carmen says she really wants to join in, but her parents, who are not strict with her otherwise, categorically reject it. Then Carmen had the idea of ??smuggling me in.

"How are you going to do that?" I asked her.

"I can do it! Let me do it! I just have to get to the PC of Papa's secretary, if he isn't there, I'll just write you on the list, nobody buckles that! "

Well and today it happened! I have the invitation. I've already made everything clear for my parents, I'm sleeping with a friend. The most important thing at the moment is my costume. I was at a costume rental. The princess costume I chose fits perfectly, but is far too expensive. Carmen gave me half of it, otherwise it would have been over.

"On one condition," she said. "You tell me every little detail afterwards. I want to know everything. Everything! No matter how piquant it is."

Of course I promised her that. So I have the dress and now I can hardly wait. My friend Petra has been initiated into our plan. She gave me the alibi and I will also change with her. From there I take the taxi to the festival. I am so terribly excited.

The week goes far too slowly. My parents even notice my restlessness and I have to come up with an excuse why I am so restless. But now it's done. I packed my stuff and cycle to my friend Petra.

"Are you sure you really want to go there? I don't know about your sex experience, except for what you told me, so you're definitely not an expert! "

I think for a moment before answering Petra: "Of course you are absolutely right and basically it is a totally crazy idea to go there. In truth, it was Carmen's idea, but now everything has been regulated to such an extent that I actually can't help it. So don't make me doubt. And if I am completely honest, I have to admit that the thought of this wicked festival makes me really fucker. "

" Well, I can understand that it makes you fucker, but I still admire your courage. Let's start to make you right . "

We spend the next few hours trying on, hairdressing, applying make-up, discarding everything and starting from scratch, etc. But in the end I am standing in front of the mirror.

"As a little girl, I always dreamed of such a dress."

"Me too," enthuses Petra. "I always wanted to be a princess too! Have you ever checked your watch? Your taxi has to be here at any moment. "

I jump up and grab my handbag and my coat when the doorbell rings. The taxi driver looks surprised, but then he realizes that I want to go to a costume party. As I give him the address, he whistles approvingly and drives off.

It is not far from Othmarschen to Blankenese, the traffic is limited and after about 15 minutes the car turns into the property entrance. The tires crunch on the gravel path. It is already dark outside and the tall trees next to the driveway look ghostly in the light of the path lighting.

Suddenly it gets light. The gravel path winds around a fountain, but the water feature is now not switched on in the cold season. Mom was right - a palace! A huge entrance area with round columns, a few steps leading to the double-leaf entrance door and everything bathed in bright light. The car comes to a standstill, a liveried man (is that called a servant?) Opens the door and helps me get out.

"Along there, please." He shows me the way to the stairs. I walk up the stairs like a real princess.

Another gentleman, this time in a dark suit, asks me for my invitation. He glances at it and compares my name with a list that he has on a clipboard.

"Ms. Juliane Kerper, ah yes, there I have you. If you had the kindness over there to go to the cloakroom, they'll take your coat off."

Another gentleman in the cloakroom, also dressed in a dark suit, is waiting for the guests. He helps me out of my coat and then looks at me briefly.

"A wonderful costume, ma'am, if I may allow myself the remark. Please follow the other guests to the left in the side wing, there is our large hall. I wish the merciful Miss a pleasant evening. "

With a friendly smile he shows me the direction. Through a wide open portal I get into the hall. There are covered small tables with chairs everywhere. On the sides I also see small bar tables and in between always Again comfortable armchairs and two-seat sofas, where guests have settled down to chat. The guests are having a good time everywhere. I look at the sometimes very elaborate costumes. A wonderful, colorful picture of cheerful exuberance.

I discover a gallery supported by thick round columns above the entrance portal, but it seems to be empty, in any case I cannot see any guests up there. I turn around, on the other side of the room, several wide doors are open. I stroll there and see what is hidden there in the neighboring room.

I'm speechless. The biggest buffet I have ever seen, not even on TV. The long table overflows with all kinds of delicacies. The water in my mouth runs down.

I look further and see a large bar where a liveried bartender is preparing drinks that are carried away by eager and very pretty girls. The girls wear all the bunny costumes that are reminiscent of the Playboy bunnies. However, instead of the usual panties with the pompom on the bottom, they wear very daring short skirts. Very sexy!

Next to the bar, on a long table, there are numerous baskets, all of which are numbered. I cannot explain what that means at the moment.

I stroll back into the great hall and look around to see if I see someone I know. A bunny comes by and I take a glass of sparkling wine, or is it champagne? From her tray. I take a sip of my drink, it tastes wonderful.

A Spanish grandee is approaching me. He wears a ruff, a doublet, tights and high, soft boots. A handsome young man, I think. My eyes slide over his costume and get stuck on his tights. The pants are so tight that their gender is precisely molded and can be clearly seen. I can see his sack with the two eggs in it and also his member, which seems quite large to me. However, I lack the sufficient possibilities of comparison, strictly speaking, I only know the Internet pictures and an occasional scintillating look at my father in the bathroom or my brother.

"May I keep you company?" He asks me politely. "My name is Robert von Gauding."

I smile at him: "Of course you can. My name is Juliane Kerper, but please call me Jule and, better still, do without the formal you. "

" But very much Jule, provided you call me Robert, or better still Bobby, my nickname. "

We clink glasses with our glasses and take a sip. He looks me in the eye.

"I am a Spanish Grande and after we have decided to forego all the formalities and have a chat, can I surely rob them of a little kiss?"

"But sir!" I reply, indignantly, "but that shouldn't be , we don't even know each other yet. "

Ignoring my objection, he takes my glass and places it on the table next to us. He reaches around my waist and pulls me towards him. Before I can still resist, he playfully touches my lips with his and gives me a gentle kiss.

"Thank you very much, lady. Your lips are soft and promising with a hint of champagne flavor. I think we should repeat that again, but maybe a little more intensely. "

" Bobby, please, "I end our game. "I know well that tonight should also have an erotic component, but not now?"

"Why not? Besides, I just want a kiss."

He doesn't wait for another answer from me. His hand, which is still on my hip, pulls me back to him and this time he holds me tight. His open lips press against mine. I feel his tongue come towards me and I let it in. Our tongues play with each other tenderly. It tastes of champagne and erotic. I feel him press his abdomen against my stomach because he's a bit bigger than me. He rubs against me and I can feel his member, it seems hard to me. Hard? Isn't he going to? There is no doubt. What I feel rubbing against me is an erection. Gosh, what a stupid word. He has a hard on! Surprisingly, I am not uncomfortable with this certainty

Bobby lets go of me and looks at me with a bright smile.

"That was a beautiful kiss, Jule, we have to repeat it soon and deepen it a bit."

What does he mean by deepening? I can imagine that and I get red cheeks. I look at his tights. His cock is stiff. Even I can see the plump acorn through the thin fabric. Bobby follows my gaze. His stand does not seem embarrassing to him.

"Do you like that?" he asks cheekily.

I have no words, but I nod as if I was in a trance. He grabs my hand and leads it to his manhood. I feel his tail twitch.

"You want to get to know HIM, am I right?"

I nod again. What a stupid cow I am to show the first best guy how hot I am. Well, it's too late now and that's why I'm here. Still, I shouldn't have nodded, I'm annoyed. Before our fumbling becomes dangerous, a whistle sounds over the loudspeakers and then someone begins to speak:

"My dear friends, dear guests. I am happy to welcome you to our annual costume party. "

Obviously the host who gives the welcoming speech in flowery words. I only listen with half an ear because I am still a bit irritated by Bobby and my feelings. Bobby's hand lies also no longer on my hip, but caresses my bottom, through my heavy dress with the many ruffles and petticoats underneath.

I will not tolerate anything like this here, everything must be done on a lustful, voluntary basis. Unlike the previous festivals, this time I will make the amount of the donation that I usually send to a non-profit organization dependent on you. For every bra, panties for women or men that are given at the bar, I increase the donation by 100 €. You will have noticed the baskets next to the bar. You will find a personal number on your invitation. All items of clothing handed in will be kept in their personal basket. The bunnies will be constantly on the move in the hall and will also collect other items of clothing. If you give the young women your personal number, these items of clothing will also be placed in your basket. A word about the bunnies. These young ladies have a job to do here and do not serve the pleasure of my guests. Nevertheless, they are allowed to participate in everything as long as they fulfill their actual duties sufficiently. I could imagine that after the initial rush, the amount of clothes dropped will decrease significantly. But the same applies here: The young women are not prostitutes, they are not fair game! Enough of the long speech, I wish you lots and lots of fun tonight. " The young women are not prostitutes, they are not fair game! Enough of the long speech, I wish you lots and lots of fun tonight. " The young women are not prostitutes, they are not fair game! Enough of the long speech, I wish you lots and lots of fun tonight. "

So yes. The rumors are correct. Today's party will be a huge orgy - and I'm in! Am i afraid Hm, yes, a little bit. Am i hot Yes, and how!

"Come and get something from the buffet, I need strengthening, it will be a stressful night:"

Accompanied by Bobby, we grab a bite at the buffet and wash everything down with champagne Band only plays cuddly music. I slide into his arms and sway with him to the rhythm of the music. Bobby's hand is unabashed and visible to everyone on my bottom. Again I feel his hard cock.

"Do you feel my excitement?" He whispers in my ear.

"Yes, and how."

"Do you like it?"

"Yes, it excites me."

"I would like to feel your excitement."

"It doesn't work now, but later - maybe. How would you do it, I mean, how would you want to feel my excitement? "

" Oh, nothing easier than that. My hand would crawl under your skirts. It would find your panties and make your way underneath. I would feel if you are wearing a fur or you are shaved I would search for your labia and feel their shape and size I would split them with your finger and penetrate your slit I would feel your wetness and penetrate deep inside with your finger I would spread your juices on your clit and feel if it is already swollen. "

"Listen to Bobby!"

"Why,

"Yes and how. But I can hardly stop it if you whisper something into my ear. I also flow away. My panties are probably already wet. "

" Come on, let's take a break from dancing. I could also use some of the delicious lobster. "

Bobby obviously tries to reduce our excitement a bit and save it for later. We fill our plates and look at the guests on the dance floor. There is heavy swuffling and cuddling. Men and women, from young to old, enjoy the erotic atmosphere. But everyone has enough discipline to limit the fumbling to the outside. I look at the clock, just before eleven. It grumbles in my stomach, I'm nervous. As I watch the dancing people, Bobby steps behind me. He hugs me and embraces me with his arms. Without scruples, he grabs my breasts with both hands.

"What cute, horny tits. I want to suck your nipples now. "

A shiver runs through my body. At the same time, I feel something like anger about Bobby's audacity.

"Jule! What are you doing? "

I know the voice that startles me all too well. My mother! Damn it, what is she doing here. I free myself from Bobby's hug and turn around. In front of me is an angry Madame Pompadour, with a teasing beauty mark on the cheek, a daring cleavage from which the big breasts gush out. Mom seems to be wearing a corset because her torso and waist are remarkably slim.

"Mom I, uh .."

"Don't stutter around here. How do you get here

"I have an invitation, so I can be here."

"Good thing your dad hasn't spotted you yet. You have to go home immediately. And anyway, where is the costume from and how does the guy get to publicly grab your breasts? Really! "

" Please mom. Let me stay here. "

An excited discussion follows. Unfortunately, the guests standing nearby also get the mother - daughter dispute. It is really embarrassing. To make matters worse, my dad also shows up here. It is only when I point out to the two that this festival is going to be very erotic and I am also surprised that my parents are here at all. Still, I have to accept Papa's final decision that I have to leave at noon. Such a crap!

My parents disappear into the fray. I look around for Bobby, but he quickly went far. A look at the clock: It's 11:45 a.m. Well, it's not even worth looking for Bobby. I take a glass of champagne and throw it down out of anger. Immediately I'll take another one, which I drink a little more slowly. I watch the hustle and bustle a little. Mom is standing in a corner of the room. Her beau is about her age, he wears a devil costume. He has buried his face in her breasts, pressed up through the corset, and she seems to be enjoying it. I find dad on the dance floor. He has a young thing in his arm (well maybe a little older than me). She is disguised as a harem lady. Everything is transparent and airy. She's not on the dance floor, rather Papa wears it because she has her legs wrapped around his waist and so Papa weighs himself to the music. I bet he still fucks her, it goes through my head, but immediately I'm ashamed of my thoughts. Not that I don't think the two of them will fuck, but because of the word "fuck", I don't normally use and think such terms. But today I like the word and also some others that are considered dirty.

I make my way, I pass the mighty pillars that rise to the ceiling and carry the gallery halfway up. I leave the room through the portal, I look around and look for the cloakroom when I discover a door that is marked with the word "gallery". Nobody pays attention to me. The door opens, I slip through and climb over up the stairs to the gallery. Another door blocks my way. This can also be opened and I am on the gallery. It is like an inner balcony, about 2m wide. Between the columns there is a wall about 80cm high. A single armchair stands around here, I walk past him to the edge of the wall in the corner of the gallery. Here I'm half protected from looking through the door, only an attentive observer from below could see me, but everyone is too busy with himself and the other guests. My watch shows a quarter of an hour after midnight. The bunnies eagerly carry dishes from the hall. Cuddling couples are standing or sitting everywhere, I can see some exposed breasts and, over there, a young woman took her partner's cock out of her pants. It is plump and vertical like a flagpole. It is a pity that I am quite far away and details are hidden from me. yes over there a young woman took her partner's cock out of her pants. It is plump and vertical like a flagpole. It is a pity that I am quite far away and details are hidden from me. yes over there a young woman took her partner's cock out of her pants. It is plump and vertical like a flagpole. It is a pity that I am quite far away and details are hidden from me.

I try to ventilate my various skirts and petticoats a little and get under my dress with my hand. Not that easy, but it works. I find my panties that I can easily slide aside on the crotch. My researching finger immediately sinks, covered with slimy, slippery wetness between my labia and further in my hot hole. I can't help groaning. I am wet, horny and unsatisfied. It could have been such a great evening, instead I stand like a voyeur on the gallery and finger my panties.

The level of undressing in the hall is increasing. A completely naked woman is leaning over the back of a chair. It is rather stout. Her heavy breasts squeeze out from under her weight. A naked man also stands behind her and fondles her column from behind, with both hands he pulls her butt cheeks apart and then sticks his seesawing cock into her cunt.

Did I think "cunt"? "Column"? "Ass"? "Tail"? I'm crazy! My little finger glides back and forth in my pussy like a sewing machine. I moan, I'm horny and I would now like to be the woman over the arm of the chair.

A sound! That was the pawing of this chair up here. Rustling. Damn, I didn't hear the door open. I pull my hand out from under my princess dress, turn behind my pillar and try to catch a glimpse of what's happening near me.

I catch my breath. An old man, a general, at least he wears an old-fashioned uniform with many medals and golden strands sitting in the armchair. He is positioned in such a way that he can look over the wall and at the most shows his head from below. This is better because his pants and underpants hang on his ankles. He holds his limp tail in his hand and massages the glans. He watches the fuck in the hall, but his tail remains limp. Although his thing is not stiff, it is of a decent size, the glans looks out curiously and is not covered by the foreskin. Up close I watch a man, albeit an old man, caressing his cock. He looks nice, but also frustrated. I still think the situation is awesome and therefore send my hand back under my skirts. I am careless and therefore my handbag slides off my shoulder and falls on the floor.

The old man reacts quickly and covers his shame with his shirt.

"Who's there? Who has the cheek to watch me secretly? "

Despite the degrading situation, his voice is firm and composed. I come behind my pillar. I'm ashamed that I got horny on him. In a shaky voice I say:" I that's it. I apologize, I'm ashamed, but I can't help it. I was here first. "

The general looks at me: "Look, who do we have there? A princess. A princess and an old general. "

" I'm sure you're mad at me now? "

"Oh princess, I'm not angry with you, at most I'm angry with my own carelessness. As you can see, even an old general is not immune to embarrassing mistakes. Now I'm sitting here with my trousers on my ankles and covering my shame with great difficulty, and I hope a pretty princess doesn't laugh at me. "

" I would never laugh at her. "

"Then be nice and turn around so I can restore my dignity and put my trousers back on."

I hesitate. I just look at him. He's up here for the same reason as me. He watches the horny couples and he is sharp himself, albeit with little success.

"Well what is it? Turn around!"

"I don't want to," I hear myself say.

"You don't want to? What do you want?"

"I want to, yes I want to ..."

"Don't stutter around. You want to continue enjoying my degrading sight!"

"No, I don't mean that, I want ... I want to see him!"

Now it's out. I feel the blood shoot into my face and I am definitely blazing red.

"You mean you want to see him? Who him? " He hesitates. "You mean him who is hid under my shirt?"

I nod.

"Princess! I'm an old guy and as you have seen, it is not far with him. Look over the wall and you will see her, as they should be, not as limp as mine. "

"Nevertheless. Those down there are far away. I want to see him up close. "

"The fruit of a pretty princess like you is surely already picked by a handsome prince, or are you still a virgin?"

I shake my head.

"Well. Then you have a tail, excuse the expression, but that's what it means, already seen, in your hand and already in your pussy. "

"In my pussy, but not seen and not in my hand."

"How is that supposed to work? Tell me if you dare. I'm a good listener."

I stand in front of a half-naked, old man and I intend to tell him my most intimate thing, but I feel like I have to do it. He gave up his male weakness before me, though involuntarily, so I owe him something.

"It was at a party. We had all drunk. The crush of all the girls in my school brought me to the dance floor to dance. A slow piece of music. He pulls me in and cuddles with me as we move slowly to the music. I can feel his hard thing he's rubbing against me. He has one hand on my buttocks, the other squeezes between our torsos and feels my breasts, my hard nipples. He lets go of me, takes my hand and pulls me behind him. I know what he wants and what is happening now. I want it too. We end up in a room with a bed. We take off our shoes and slip under the covers. It is dark in the room. We smooch. I feel his hand under my skirt, it pulls on my panties. I lift my bottom and it pulls it down to me. His hand fumbles on my pussy. I'm very wet down there. He takes his hand away and fiddles with his pants, he rolls on me between my thighs. He directs something hard to my entrance. He pushes into me, slides in effortlessly, a powerful push and a sharp pain. I am no longer a virgin, but I had imagined it differently. He fucks me, please excuse me, so he penetrates me rhythmically, only a few times. He groans, rears up and I feel that he injects his semen into me. I didn't think of protection or children. The fear comes later, but I was lucky. His cock slackens, he pulls it out, he kisses me and says it wasn't bad. In the dark he pulls up his pants and leaves the room. I'm very wet down there. He takes his hand away and fiddles with his pants, he rolls on me between my thighs. He directs something hard to my entrance. He pushes into me, slides in effortlessly, a powerful push and a sharp pain. I am no longer a virgin, but I had imagined it differently. He fucks me, please excuse me, so he penetrates me rhythmically, only a few times. He groans, rears up and I feel that he injects his semen into me. I didn't think of protection or children. The fear comes later, but I was lucky. His cock slackens, he pulls it out, he kisses me and says it wasn't bad. In the dark he pulls up his pants and leaves the room. I'm very wet down there. He takes his hand away and fiddles with his pants, he rolls on me between my thighs. He directs something hard to my entrance. He pushes into me, slides in effortlessly, a powerful push and a sharp pain. I am no longer a virgin, but I had imagined it differently. He fucks me, please excuse me, so he penetrates me rhythmically, only a few times. He groans, rears up and I feel that he injects his semen into me. I didn't think of protection or children. The fear comes later, but I was lucky. His cock slackens, he pulls it out, he kisses me and says it wasn't bad. In the dark he pulls up his pants and leaves the room. he rolls on me between my thighs. He directs something hard to my entrance. He pushes into me, slides in effortlessly, a powerful push and a sharp pain. I am no longer a virgin, but I had imagined it differently. He fucks me, please excuse me, so he penetrates me rhythmically, only a few times. He groans, rears up and I feel that he injects his semen into me. I didn't think of protection or children. The fear comes later, but I was lucky. His cock slackens, he pulls it out, he kisses me and says it wasn't bad. In the dark he pulls up his pants and leaves the room. he rolls on me between my thighs. He directs something hard to my entrance. He pushes into me, slides in effortlessly, a powerful push and a sharp pain. I am no longer a virgin, but I had imagined it differently. He fucks me, please excuse me, so he penetrates me rhythmically, only a few times. He groans, rears up and I feel that he injects his semen into me. I didn't think of protection or children. The fear comes later, but I was lucky. His cock slackens, he pulls it out, he kisses me and says it wasn't bad. In the dark he pulls up his pants and leaves the room. a strong push and a sharp pain. I am no longer a virgin, but I had imagined it differently. He fucks me, please excuse me, so he penetrates me rhythmically, only a few times. He groans, rears up and I feel that he injects his semen into me. I didn't think of protection or children. The fear comes later, but I was lucky. His cock slackens, he pulls it out, he kisses me and says it wasn't bad. In the dark he pulls up his pants and leaves the room. a strong push and a sharp pain. I am no longer a virgin, but I had imagined it differently. He fucks me, please excuse me, so he penetrates me rhythmically, only a few times. He groans, rears up and I feel that he injects his semen into me. I didn't think of protection or children. The fear comes later, but I was lucky. His cock slackens, he pulls it out, he kisses me and says it wasn't bad. In the dark he pulls up his pants and leaves the room. I didn't think of protection or children. The fear comes later, but I was lucky. His cock slackens, he pulls it out, he kisses me and says it wasn't bad. In the dark he pulls up his pants and leaves the room. I didn't think of protection or children. The fear comes later, but I was lucky. His cock slackens, he pulls it out, he kisses me and says it wasn't bad. In the dark he pulls up his pants and leaves the room.

That was my first and only time. I didn't see anything, just felt it. Today everything should be different, today I wanted everything at once. It did not work. My parents discovered me and sent me home - now I'm here. "

The general listened attentively.

"I understand, so I'm your only possible replacement for your missed adventure. You won't believe it, my situation is different and yet the same. I am an old man, albeit a sprightly one. Old men can no longer do as they used to. I'm having trouble making him tough. I thought this was a good place for one last great adventure. I was down there, drunk with craving. A pretty mistress with a corset and big boobs was willing and ready. I fingered her horny, dripping cunt and she moaned and twisted in her lust. Then I opened my pants and got my cock out. She blew him adorable. I watched her work on it in her beautiful blow mouth. She had such a cute little beauty mark on her cheek. The woman was pure eroticism, I couldn't have hit it better. All around me was fucked and this beautiful woman sucks on my spanking. Well, what can I say, I couldn't get him up. At some point she gave up. With her bare abdomen and her thighs spread, she lay down on a table and some guy who came by with a stiff cock took her and fucked her. She squeaked like a stabbed pig and I pulled my pants up and went to the gallery in shame. I didn't want to give up and thought with a little time and patience I can get him up. Nothing. Instead, I embarrass myself a second time. All around me was fucked and this beautiful woman sucks on my spanking. Well, what can I say, I couldn't get him up. At some point she gave up. With her bare abdomen and her thighs spread, she lay down on a table and some guy who came by with a stiff cock took her and fucked her. She squeaked like a stabbed pig and I pulled my pants up and went to the gallery in shame. I didn't want to give up and thought with a little time and patience I can get him up. Nothing. Instead, I embarrass myself a second time. All around me was fucked and this beautiful woman sucks on my spanking. Well, what can I say, I couldn't get him up. At some point she gave up. With her bare abdomen and her thighs spread, she lay down on a table and some guy who came by with a stiff cock took her and fucked her. She squeaked like a stabbed pig and I pulled my pants up and went to the gallery in shame. I didn't want to give up and thought with a little time and patience I can get him up. Nothing. Instead, I embarrass myself a second time. With her bare abdomen and her thighs spread, she lay down on a table and some guy who came by with a stiff cock took her and fucked her. She squeaked like a stabbed pig and I pulled my pants up and went to the gallery in shame. I didn't want to give up and thought with a little time and patience I can get him up. Nothing. Instead, I embarrass myself a second time. With her bare abdomen and her thighs spread, she lay down on a table and some guy who came by with a stiff cock took her and fucked her. She squeaked like a stabbed pig and I pulled my pants up and went to the gallery in shame. I didn't want to give up and thought with a little time and patience I can get him up. Nothing. Instead, I embarrass myself a second time.

And now you want to see him. Want me further embarrass. "

" No I will not. I just want to see him. You do not need to be ashamed and not be embarrassed. "

"On one condition: I can see your princess

plum !" I only nod and he slowly pulls his shirt from his pubic. He spreads his legs apart as far as the trousers on the ankles allow. A big sack with heavy eggs hangs there. His limp tail, whose acorn is not covered by the foreskin, dangles above it. He lifts his tail a little and releases it again. He immediately hangs between his thighs again.

"May I touch him?"

The old man nods. I bend down to him. Reach for the limp tail. He feels good, tall, just not woken up yet. I take his sack in my hand. It more than fills my palm. I press it and feel the eggs. I squeeze the eggs, which move slightly back and forth in the sack. With one hand I play with his balls while I massage the tail with the other. I pull the foreskin forward and can just cover the glans, when I let go I look curiously out into the open again with one eye. I repeat the game a few times. I have the impression that the tail would be bigger and a little firmer. I bend down to him. The acorn is right in front of my face. I sniff, but the tail is completely clean and odorless.

Should I. I have seen it many times on the Internet. I open my mouth and pick it up there. I suck on the Nille and play around with my tongue while I continue to press and knead his fat balls, but now with both hands.

My general groans. I seem to do it well, he likes it and I like it. With dedication I suck and suck and I feel success. It grows. It is incredible, it is growing. I am proud. According to his description, it was my mother who blew his tail earlier. How awesome she is, as he described it, she is fucked senseless tonight.

"Princess, you are doing this wonderfully. Can you feel my old cock growing and thriving. Do not stop! It's been a long time since my fat man was in the mouth of such a pretty, young woman. Almost still a virgin and blowing like a goddess. Princess, what are you doing with an old general. He hadn't been that stiff for a long time. Oh yes, oh yes, squeeze my balls. Hey you rascal, you bite my acorn? Oh my god that's awesome. Just a little bit more. It's so big that it won't fit in your sweet mouth anymore. "

The general is right, I think. His mighty cock has grown into a giant. If I try to put it in my mouth I have to choke. Sucking the plump acorn is a lot hotter anyway. I make my mouth very tight and fuck him at least the upper part of his cock. I try to grip the shaft with my hand, but I can't close it completely, it's too thick for that. How wonderfully hard the thing is now. I take it out of my mouth and look at it: it is large, hard, long with a curious, plump acorn. The shaft has thick, pulsating veins. It never fits into my tight cunt, I think.

"Princess, now you have to keep your promise. Show me your most secret! "

I stand and collect my skirts so I can lift them up. It succeeds with difficulty. My abdomen is right in front of his face.

"Hold on to your skirts, little princess, I'll take off your panties."

He doesn't seem to be expecting an answer, and without further ado he

slides down my panties, where he still helps me to get out of them. "Now spread your thighs ! "

I willingly obey him. His hand slides up between my thighs and touches my crotch.

"What a cuddly, soft fur you have there!"

He caresses my hairy pussy and gently cuddles through the hair. Then he cuts my pronounced labia and wets his fingers with my wet.

"Such a wet, dripping, young Fickfotzchen. What a gift for an old man! "

My general is right, I am running out. And I am so horny! I enjoy the treatment of my cunt by the experienced fingers of this old man. I take a look at his cock which is vertically upwards He stands like a one and does not start to collapse again. Fingering my wet hole seems to make him even hotter. After he has extensively explored and fingered my labia, my clit and the depth of my cunt he pulls me closer to him so he can get his face in. He buries his face in my bush and tries to reach my clit with his tongue.

"Princess it doesn't work that way. Come on my kitten, get on the armchair and lean forward. Support yourself on the wall with your hands. Let your skirts fall down, I'll dive under them. "

Just a moment later I'm standing on the edge of the armchair upholstery, leaning forward looking at the fucking guests below me. The general has disappeared behind me with my whole upper body under my skirts. I feel his breath between my thighs, fingers that open my labia and then a warm tongue that seems to be

tasting my juices. The tongue runs through my slit, back and forth . "You taste beguiling, you make an old man drunk with pleasure "I hear his voice muffled under my dress.

Again his fingers grab my labia and pull them apart. His tongue fucks my hole and I moan, filled with unknown feelings. Then his tongue finds the clit of my clit. A lustful shower makes me tremble, I can hardly stand and am afraid of falling. I pull myself together and enjoy how he alternately licks my clit and nibbles on him. I know what it feels like to finger his wet cunt and get an orgasm, but what is now happening under my skirt cannot be compared to anything.

A warm tongue massages my clit and nothing under me but fucking couples. I look around the room searching. Yes, not far from me I see my mom. Your Pompadur costume has disappeared. She is naked except for her shoes. She is lying on her back on one of the tables. She has a full, buxom figure. Her big, soft boobs are boobs - no breasts, hanging on the left and right side. They are adorned by dark areolas and stiff, cherry-sized nipples. At the head of the head are two young men whose stiff cocks she wanks with her hands. On the other hand another stands between her thighs and eagerly fucks her smooth, shaved cunt. A young woman approaches, naked like everyone else. She is flat-chested, but a lush black bush grows between her thighs. She climbs on the table. At this very moment one of the young cocks starts to squirt like a fountain. Some of his cargo lands on Mama's breasts, some on the white tablecloth. Now the other tail is spitting its load. A few drops land on Mama's face. Mom releases the tails after they are unloaded. The young woman with the thick bush climbs over my mother and, in position 69, presses her bush into her face. I can't see it exactly, but I can tell from the young woman's expression that Mama's tongue is doing the right thing on her cunt. Suddenly the fucker rears up between Mom's thighs. He pulls his bulging tube out of the cunt and pushes it into the young woman's mouth. Not a second later I hear his cry up to the gallery, when he drops his semen into the young woman's mouth. She tries to swallow, but a few white drops swell from the corners of her mouth.

I will never forget the sight of my fucking, licking mother. I don't know if the sight repels me - no, it actually excites me more.

I don't notice how loud I moan now. My pussy contracts and a huge orgasm floods me. I am shaking and just barely prevent falling. It slowly subsides. My general continues to lick until I get off my armchair with trembling knees.

"Well princess, was that nice for you?"

"Oh yes general, I've never had such a wonderful orgasm."

I go to him and finally take off his pants, then I snuggle up to him and unbutton his uniform jacket.

"What are you doing there little one?"

"I'll take you off, I want to have her completely naked."

For a moment he is speechless and I continue to undress him. I drop the clothes carelessly and a moment later he sits naked in front of me in the armchair. I look at his wrinkled but sinewy body, which is crowned in the middle by a still gorgeous stiff tail. I turn around and ask him to open my dress at the back. With my costume it is all a bit more complex, but finally I stand naked in front of him I turn so that he can look at me from all sides.

"You have a wonderful bubble butt and pretty firm tits with curious, small but stiff nipples. Come on let me feel your wonderful ass!"

I bend forward a bit and present him with my already-praised bottom. He grabs with both hands, pats, strokes and kneads him and when I spread my thighs a little he grabs my pussy from behind and lets two fingers penetrate my hole. I hold still as he fucks me with my fingers. It is not easy for me to keep still, but the compulsion to do so increases my desire. When he wants to stop, I ask him to continue because another orgasm is already announcing in my young plum. I moan loudly when it shakes violently again.

"I have never seen a woman who gets such violent orgasms in quick succession. Look at my hand I got all wet. There aren't many women who get wet, sometimes squirting orgasms. "

" That has never happened to me before. Maybe it's because I'm so terribly horny. I'm ashamed that I can't get enough. "

"Kitty, don't be ashamed, on the contrary, you give me great pleasure."

"General, do you think her member is too big for me?"

"What do you think. Yes it is big, but it fits, believe me. It is also my cock and not a sterile member! Does your question mean that you want to be fucked by me? "

" Oh yes! That means it. Now right now. "

The general gets up, his tail points at me. He directs me to the armchair and I lean over the back. In this position my mother was fucked earlier. The general spreads my thighs and pulls my buttocks apart. Then I feel his big pipe knock on my entrance. He reaches for my cunt and opens my labia. He skillfully directs the tip of his tail in front of the wide open hole. A little pressure and I feel my cunt stretched. I was expecting pain, but under his pressure he penetrated my hole almost playfully.

"The acorn is already in your sweet cunt. Did it hurt?"

"No no. Fuck me! Push him in. I know you don't splash after three thrusts. Make me quick and violent. Your kitten is a horny cat that needs it right, that needs to be fucked properly. "

My coarse words cheer him on and with powerful thrusts he serves my hungry column. I can't look down in this position, but that doesn't matter. I'm getting fucked like a real horny woman and not like a schoolgirl, I scream and moan uncontrollably.

My orgasm subsides and I ask my lover to let me ride him. He pulls his hard out of my pussy and lies on the floor. I stand wide-legged above him and wait a moment to take a look at my dilated, swollen cunt. I crouch over his tail and direct it in front of my opening, then I sit down slowly and enjoy how his tube penetrates me. At first slowly, but then faster and more impatiently I increase my movements to a perfection ride. My lust is huge and my general groans and groans under more.

"Before I get it I'll tell you, princess. Then you get off and put my cock in your mouth. You should know what freshly sprayed male seeds taste like. "

I nod and ride on. The spanking in my hole gives me endless pleasure. It feels like something alive in me. My quick ride shows success and again a wet orgasm shakes me. My general, however, barely gives me time to let the orgasm die away.

"I'm kitten so far! I will inject right away. Get my juice! "

I get off his cock and slide back onto his legs to put the fat one in his mouth. I reach for his shaft with both hands, I take the plump acorn in my mouth. I taste my own pussy taste. I eagerly move my mouth up and down as I lick the glans. That is too much for him. With a loud groan he pushes his pelvis up and his spank penetrates deep into my throat, then I feel the warm sauce squirt out of him. It doesn't stop, more and more splashes fill my mouth. I try to swallow the slightly salty sauce as much as possible, but my chin runs down a bit anyway.

"How cute you look, princess. Heated with red cheeks, a little pumped out but freshly fucked happy. Some sperm hangs on your chin, which makes you look a bit ordinary, which is a wonderful contradiction to your youth. Come to me I want to lick your chin clean. "

I snuggle into his arm and enjoy how he gently licks me cleanly. We stroke each other and enjoy our intimacy and just gained familiarity. After a few minutes we get up and help each other each other in the costumes. My hairstyle is ruined and can't be saved, but that doesn't bother me.

Arm in arm we stand by the wall and look down on the still lively hustle and bustle. In the middle of the hall, several of the tables were pushed together in a long row. Naked women lie close together with spread thighs on the tables and present the men with their horny, open cracks, young girls, mature women and older women are mixed there. Small plump breasts, large breasts and heavy, soft sagging breasts. Shaved, smooth slits next to bulging labia, thick black, fuzzy bushes next to cleanly trimmed pussies. A long puss parade of every old and every appearance. The men who stand between their thighs present their stiff erect legs. Short, thick tails next to thin stems, huge spankings with heavy bags, and pretty shaped,

As if on command, they penetrate the cunts in front of them and begin to push them hard. Some men reach for the tits to knead them and twirl the nipples, others grab the thighs of the women and lie on their shoulders in order to be able to penetrate better.

The ramming may take a minute, then the guys let go of their horny women and pull their cocks out of the wet holes. They turn to the next willing women to sink their cocks in the holes and continue to fuck.

My eyes are looking for my parents. I find my dad who is pulling a young thing through. I almost have the impression of hearing them squeak, but of course that is deceptive, all the horny noises are too loud down there. Papa pumps vigorously into the young fuck hole and then turns to the next one after a minute with his tail wobbling. This time he has an old woman with saggy tits and thick, curly puss hair in front of him. He fucks her as intensely as the girl before. Some younger guys pull their slats out of their cunts so that they can spray hard now. They spread their load on the belly and breasts of the women in front of them. With a slack tail they step back. Fresh, waiting fuckers take their place.

After a while I find my mom too. She did not line up in the Fotzenparade. She is sitting on the lap of a man I can't see well and is rocking back and forth slightly. Without a doubt, she also has a cock in her cunt, but she must probably take some care of her pussy because she has been served a lot. So she slowly rocks on the man's lap and looks at the fucking mass in front of her.

My general, who has been holding me up to now, is as fascinated as I am about what is happening between him. His arm slid down a bit so that he can now stroke my plump ass. Meanwhile, I reached for his manliness, which I massage gently.

Would you like to join down there now? "I ask him.

No, not really. You gave me something today that is much more important to me and that I enjoyed with all the trains and you? "

" I think I like it much better here with you too. " I look at him with delight: "

Are you taking me home now?" "Of course, honey, you have to be home before your parents come."

"I was actually thinking about your home."

"Mine? You don't need more, are you so starved for sex? Don't forget I'm an old man. And what will your parents say if you aren't there are you? "

"It's not a problem with my parents, after everything I've seen today. I don't know if I'm starved, I know that I got to know something today that I haven't had enough of and that you are an old man, I know that too. But I once managed to bring their powerful friend down to life, and I succeed again after they have rested a little. And if not, then it doesn't matter, because then my general still has magic fingers and a magical tongue. "

The End.